Heartsinger

Heartsinger

KARLIJN STOFFELS

Translated by
LAURA WATKINSON

ARTHUR A. LEVINE BOOKS
An Imprint of Scholastic Inc.

All rights reserved. Published by Arthur A. Levine Books,
an imprint of Scholastic Inc., *Publishers since 1920,* by arrangement
with Em. Querido's Uitgeverij B.V., Amsterdam, the Netherlands.
SCHOLASTIC and the LANTERN LOGO are trademarks and/or
registered trademarks of Scholastic Inc.

Library of Congress Cataloging-in-Publication Data

Stoffels, Karlijn.
[Koningsdochter, zeemanslief. English]
Heartsinger / Karlijn Stoffels; translated by Laura Watkinson. — 1st ed.
p. cm.
Summary: In this meditation on various kinds of love, Mee travels across the country to the court
of the Princess Esperanza, singing the life stories of some of the people he meets.
ISBN 978-0-545-06929-8 (hardcover) — [1. Love — Fiction. 2. Voyages and travels — Fiction.]
I. Title. II. Title: Heartsinger.
PZ7.S8697He 2009
[Fic] — dc22
2008017785

ISBN-13: 978-0-545-06929-8 / ISBN-10: 0-545-06929-7

10 9 8 7 6 5 4 3 2 1   09 10 11 12 13
Printed in the U.S.A. 23
First edition, January 2009

Book design by Elizabeth B. Parisi

This book was published with the support of the Foundation
for the Production and Translation of Dutch Literature, Amsterdam.

Table of Contents

Heartsinger

The Singer of Sorrows

In the last line of dunes, on the sandy track running past the farmland, there stood a small and shabby house. The shutters were crooked, the paint had flaked from the window frames and the doors, and the thatched roof had thin patches, where the rain seeped through when the southwest wind blew.

The house had been silent and unoccupied for a long time, but one day a young family moved in, a man with his wife and their small son. No one knew where they had come from or what they were called.

The child's early years fell on deaf ears. His mother and father could not hear or speak, nor could they read or write. They conversed with each other in sign language. But by the time he was just a few months old, the little boy had mastered their language and could babble away with his hands.

The parents earned their daily bread by beachcombing. If they found something of use on the beach, they would fix it up and take it to the village market. They also sold unusual shells and the little black pearls that you sometimes find in oysters. Every day the little boy would walk along the beach for hours, hunched over as he looked for treasures left behind in the wet sand after the sea had retreated. When he was alone, he would open his mouth as wide as he could and let sounds flow from his throat, strange sounds with strange meanings, which were lost amidst the roar of the sea and the bluster of the wind.

No one in the village had ever heard the boy speak, so everyone naturally assumed that he too was a deaf-mute. On market days, he would sit with his parents and their pitiful wares, on the ground beyond the last of the shops, and stare and stare at all of the people around him, because he was a lonely child. When people came to buy the miserable pieces of flotsam, he would watch their lips to understand what they said, just as his parents did.

One day, the schoolmaster knocked at the door of their little house.

"It's time for your son to go to school," he said as he sat down at the kitchen table.

The parents watched his mouth as he spoke and when he had finished, they nodded.

"What's the boy's name?" asked the schoolmaster.

The parents just gave him a puzzled look.

The schoolmaster placed one hand on his chest. "I am the schoolmaster," he said. "That's me. And who is he?"

The parents made signs at the schoolmaster with their hands. They always addressed each other using the signs for "husband" and "wife," and the boy was simply called "you" or "you there," or sometimes "boy."

"You there, what's your name?" sighed the schoolmaster.

The boy made a sign at the schoolmaster.

"Open your mouth and speak to me," said the schoolmaster.

The boy placed one hand on his chest and opened his mouth. "Me, that's me," he said hesitantly. "The boy You-there. That's me. I am me." His voice croaked a little.

"Mee?" asked the schoolmaster. "Is that your name? Mee?"

The boy's face lit up. He nodded furiously. "Mee." He beamed at the schoolmaster.

"Mee, you're coming to school tomorrow."

Mee nodded.

"Say 'Yes, sir,'" said the schoolmaster.

"Yes, sir," rasped Mee. Then he opened his mouth wide and let out a strange sound, which could perhaps best be translated as "Hooray!"

When Mee had been at school for two years, his father developed a mysterious illness. The doctor didn't recognize the symptoms, and Mee couldn't understand his father's words either. He kept making signs in a strange language that Mee had never seen before.

Mee was ten years old when his father died in his sleep. Mee and his mother buried him together, in the dunes. The next day, Mee went to the farmer who lived on the other side of the sandy track.

"I'm coming to work for you every day after school," he said.

The farmer nodded.

Mee began right away. He emptied the slurry pit and poured the contents onto the fields; he mucked out the cowsheds and put the beets into the root cellar. And all the time he hummed a sad song for his father.

When he got home for a late supper, he put his father's chair in the shed behind the house and his own chair in his father's place, opposite his mother, so that he could look directly at her and watch her hands as they moved. The space where her hands moved was in front of her chest, and if there was anything she couldn't express with signs, she said it with her face.

The years that followed were good years for Mee. He no longer mourned the death of his father, and he hardly ever missed him either, because a new happiness had entered his life. Before, his mother's face had always looked in his father's direction. Mee would sit beside her, and he had to work out what she was saying by watching the side of her face and the movements of her arms. Now that he could look into her eyes every day — those dark, almond eyes that slanted a little, as though she were an Eastern princess — he could finally see just how sweet she was, how beautifully her small hands and her face combined to make her feelings and thoughts clear to him, how her breath came more quickly when she was anxious, and how a tear sometimes ran down her cheek when she spoke about Mee's father.

"How beautiful you are, Mother," he would sometimes say, and she would smile at him, a little sadly.

And so it was no hardship at all for Mee to put up with his difficult life. Every day he went to school with a song on his lips; he sang when he worked on the farm, and in the evening when he walked along the sand looking for useful things, his voice would ring out over the beach.

Mee could sing so well that the schoolmaster asked him to take over the daily singing lessons for the younger children. He was paid for the teaching, so he no longer had to work on the farm.

The schoolmaster instructed him in the system of musical notes and the theory of harmony, and taught him all of the ballads and rounds and nursery rhymes and springtime songs that he had ever learned himself.

"It is a great joy to hear you sing, boy," said the schoolmaster. "You could change people's lives with that gift."

And that was true. When Mee walked down the sandy track to the dunes and sang one of his songs, the farmers in the fields would start to laugh and sway, and the children who were on their way home would dance after him. They tried to hum along with Mee, but they couldn't make head or tail of the tune and they understood few of the words. When he sang for himself, Mee only ever sang in his own language. That language resembled the language that the villagers spoke, and yet it was very different. It was a translation into words of the signs that he had learned at home from his mother and father. And the music too was of a kind that no one else knew, a music that did not correspond to the theory of harmony and the system of notes that the schoolmaster had taught to Mee.

The songs certainly sounded happy, though. Mee sang about the beauty of the beach, the warmth of the sun, the curly heads of the boys and girls he taught to sing; he sang about birds and flowers, and about his mother's smile when she saw him enter the kitchen.

But that smile was never quite as radiant as it had been before, when Mee's father was still alive. And when Mee realized this, his happiness turned to sadness, and his joy to misery.

If my mother could hear me sing, he thought, *her smile would become just as radiant as it used to be. I can make all of the villagers and their children happy and joyful. None of them can keep their feet still when I sing. Why is it that my singing voice is a joy to everyone but the person I love best?*

So one day he sang for his mother. He stood before her and sang his most beautiful song. He sang about her almond eyes and her gentle mouth; about her small hands, which always spoke so sweetly to him; about her breath, which came more quickly when she was anxious; and about her straight black hair, which gleamed when the sunlight streamed into the kitchen. He sang about her slender arms, which could do so much work; about her weary legs, which made the long walk down the beach every day; and about the wonderful scent of her skin, which smelled of sea air, sweat, and roses.

The song's words and its tune were so indescribably beautiful that all the birds for miles around stopped singing as they recognized the voice of their master, that nightingale among humans, the singer Mee. Farmers laid down their pitchforks and travelers dismounted from their horses; women took their red hands from their steaming tubs of washing, and children pricked up their ears and danced around in circles. The rain that was clattering onto the roofs of the next village just dripped a few last drops here and there; the lightning shooting through the sky nearby turned tail and flashed back into the clouds. Even the waves, which usually crashed onto the beach with a loud roar, flowed back out to sea, gently murmuring.

When the song was over, Mee sat down at the kitchen table and looked at his mother. His chest was rising and falling with exertion and anticipation.

"So?" he asked her.

All was silent inside and out. The farmers stood motionless in their fields, and even the children had stopped dancing.

Mee's mother gave her son a puzzled look, as though she were asking him what on earth he had just been doing, standing there in front of her. Then she smiled, a little sadly as always, and stood up to clear the table.

Mee grabbed the pots and the pans and the plates and he threw them at the wall, every last one. Then he ran out of the house. He didn't return until deep into the night.

The years went by. The schoolmaster now gave Mee private lessons, because the local area had only a junior school. When the children were twelve and had completed their sixth year of school, they had to go out to work. Mee continued to give the children singing lessons, and he did it well. He taught them the rounds and springtime songs and ballads that the schoolmaster had taught him. But now when he was alone he sang savage songs about war and violence, about fire-breathing dragons and loathsome monsters, about cannons that reduced entire regions to ashes, and forest fires that took the lives of deer, rabbits, and songbirds. He sang in his strange half-language, and people didn't understand all of the words, but when he came by, the women would flee into their houses, the farmers would hide behind their barns and haystacks, and the children would dive into the ditches alongside the road and put their little hands over their ears.

When he came home to his mother, he would stop singing. He talked to her and smiled at her and helped her with the things that needed to be done. And when she too became sick and weak because of the same unknown ailment that had felled his father, he carried her up the attic stairs every night to her bed, and in the morning he would carry her down to a camp bed in the back room, where they never used to sit. There he would give her food and drink, wipe the sweat from her forehead when she had a fever, and bring herbs from the dunes for her pain.

But all of his care was in vain.

A few weeks after her death, he packed his things together, locked up the house, and left. He stopped at the school to say farewell to the schoolmaster.

"Where are you going, my boy?" asked the schoolmaster.

"I'm heading east," said Mee. "I have to leave the coast. The scent of the dune roses reminds me of my mother. The sight of the waves causes me pain. Even the roar of the ocean stabs my heart."

"But what are you going to live on?" asked the schoolmaster.

"I don't want anything to live on," said Mee. "I should have died in my mother's place."

The schoolmaster took a long look at Mee. He saw that the boy's sorrow was so great that he would not be able to talk him out of it. He placed his hand on Mee's shoulder. "We had an old singer of sorrows in this land," he said. "He has just died. He came from these parts. You can take over his work."

"What do I have to do?" asked Mee, who always obeyed the schoolmaster.

"At sickbeds and at funerals, after floods and mining disasters, wherever people are mourning, you must sing for them and ease their sorrow. And by doing this you can hold dear your mother's memory."

"All right," said Mee. He said farewell to his schoolmaster and headed east.

After his very first performance, at the funeral of a just and venerable landowner, his fame began to spread from mouth to mouth and from village to village. Because Mee did not merely have a magnificent voice, which first moved people to tears and then dried those tears for them, he also had a mysterious gift. As soon as he sat at a deathbed and looked upon the face of the deceased, the entire life of that person would pass in front of his eyes. Then he would sing of that life, and the relatives would recognize the story of their loved one in the melody and the strange words, and they would keep it in their hearts and be comforted.

Before long, messengers were traveling from near and far to ask the singer of sorrows to come to a funeral service, a sickbed, a flood — in short, wherever people had need of the consolation that is called mourning.

Mee came to the mountains, where snow-covered peaks glisten in the sun and the laughter of brown-tanned shepherd boys echoes through the ravines. But he did not sing about beauty and merriment. He launched into a lament about the fire that had wiped out a flock and scorched a village. And the shepherds wept.

Mee came to the forests, where soft moss covers the ground and wide-eyed deer stand still in your path. But he did not sing about beauty and merriment. He sang the praises of the count who was the owner of the forests and who had died after a long illness. And the hunters and the poachers wept.

Mee came to the marshlands, where slender boats nose their way through the reeds, where moorhens and grebes make their comical dives. But he did not sing about beauty and merriment. He bewailed the dike that had burst, flooding a dozen farms and drowning cattle and people. And the farmers and their wives wept.

And so Mee moved through the land, coming to the smallest villages and the largest cities, always heading east, with his back to the coast, where the scent of the dune roses reminded him of his dead mother, the roar of the ocean caused him pain, and the sight of the mussel beds and white-crested waves made his heart bleed, like a blade of marram grass slicing into a finger.

One day, when he was walking through the mountains, he saw something far below, sparkling in the sun. It was a golden coach drawn by two Lipizzaner horses, struggling to make its way up the steep road.

Mee came to a halt. Perhaps the coach would take him a short way. It was warm spring weather and the road was long. As the coach came closer, he could see that the coachman up front was waving furiously at him, as though he wanted to say something. He also noticed a crown with a coat of arms beneath it on the side of the coach.

Mee thought it was the coat of arms of the island across the water. It was only a small kingdom, but it possessed a great deal of wealth, and traded with all of the countries on the mainland. It was said that the king's daughter had retreated to her rooms, never to come out again so long as she lived.

Mee sat down by the side of the road and ate a piece of bread. When the coach was only two curves in the road away from him, Mee heard the coachman calling out. He thought he heard his own name.

Suddenly, one of the horses stumbled and slipped off the road. Mee ran down. He was too late. As he rounded the bend, he was just in time to see the coach, with horses and all, rolling down the mountainside. Its fall was broken halfway when it came to a stop against an old oak tree. The sawyers, shepherds, and villagers who had seen the accident came running to offer help.

With a heavy heart, Mee went on his way.

The King's Daughter

On the island across the water, there once lived a king and a queen who were always very busy. The king was occupied all day with important affairs of state and with receiving official visitors from the mainland. The queen was also kept busy by these distinguished guests, as she had to plan proper dinners and wear proper gowns and arrange all manner of other things in a proper fashion. She was so wrapped up in her activities that she did not realize she was expecting a child until her gowns no longer fitted her.

"Oh heavens," she said. And then she forgot again, because the palace seamstress had to make new, looser-fitting robes for her, and of course they all needed to be tried on, and the queen already had so much on her mind as it was.

The King's Daughter

The king's daughter was born during an important banquet. Kings and diplomats from the lands across the water were attending the feast. The queen was keeping an eye on the young serving girls, who would still occasionally serve the food from the wrong side of the guests. She watched like a hawk, checking to see that the crystal knife rests and wine glasses had been polished and the golden bowls for the fish bones had been clipped to each of the fish plates.

Just as the guests were finishing the first course, the queen let out a loud shriek, but it was drowned out by the clink of glasses as a toast was made. The king was the only one who noticed, and he gave his wife a brief look of concern.

The tiny princess slid smoothly out from under the queen's skirts, landing, without too much of a bump, on the carpet of the dining hall. All by herself, she curled up in a damask napkin that had slipped from a guest's lap. And then, exhausted by her adventure, she fell asleep.

"Do you feel better now, my dear?" asked the king.

"I really haven't the faintest idea what it was," said the queen.

The next morning, the queen noticed that the proper gown for breakfast with the distinguished guests, which the palace seamstress had just made for her, was too large and really did not fit her any longer. It was only then that she saw where the problem was, or rather, where the problem no longer was.

"The baby!" she cried.

As soon as the king's daughter two floors below heard her mother's voice, she too began to cry out in her damask napkin, and she was soon found by the footmen who were laying the tables for breakfast.

The king's daughter, who was named Esperanza after a queen across the water, grew up as she had been born: on her own. Oh, Esperanza wanted for nothing. She was dressed in little silk clothes, rather than a damask napkin, and she was given delicious food and drink and her sheets were of the softest cambric.

But there was no mother to feed her mouthful by mouthful and no father to pick her up and whirl her around in the air. The king and queen were busy with important things. A king who has to write speeches for heads of state has no patience for listening to an infant's babbling. And a queen who must wear proper gowns finds the fidgeting and dribbling of a newborn baby most improper.

With no one paying her any attention, the lonely little princess felt as though the milk she drank had no taste and the bread she ate had no salt. Once she learned to walk, the grass of the palace gardens looked dull. The warbling of the songbirds among the faded leaves of the trees sounded monotonous and lackluster. Stiff little rabbits hopped across her path, wooden and joyless. By day the sun gave off chilly little beams of light, and at night the moon hung in the sky like the pallid yolk of a leftover egg.

One day, Esperanza, all on her own as usual, was taking a little walk around the palace gardens. She was eating an apple that had neither crunch nor flavor. In the distance, by the palace wall, she heard laughing and talking, and she walked toward the sound.

The three-year-old daughter of the gatekeeper was standing in the middle of the lawn. She was wearing a bright pink dress and spinning around and around. *Pink,* thought the princess in amazement. *Why not the usual dullness?*

And then she saw that the whole scene before her eyes was in color. The gatekeeper's wife was wearing a light blue skirt with little dots and she was hanging out colorful washing. The gatekeeper himself was in yellow clogs and had a red handkerchief on his head to protect him from the sun. And the sun, yes, the sun stood like a fiery ball in the sky, warming and illuminating the three happy people below.

"Look at me! Look at me!" cried the little girl, spinning around. The gatekeeper and his wife ran over to her.

"Yes, I can see you!" cried the gatekeeper.

"Can't you spin around beautifully!" cried his wife. The little girl stopped spinning and burst out laughing.

The gatekeeper's family disappeared inside the gatehouse, and then the colors went out again. The grass was as dull as it always had been, and the sun trickled down its watery little beams of light.

Esperanza ran back to the palace. She raced up the stairs two steps at a time and went straight to the bedroom in her own wing of the building.

"Somebody has to look at me," she babbled feverishly to herself. "Somebody has to look at me. And if nobody wants to look at me, then I'll just have to do it myself."

She sat down in front of the mirror and looked at herself. She didn't really like what she saw. Her straight black hair was dull, her dress was drab, and her mouth was a bloodless pale pink. Her eyes were the color of a deep dark ditch when it rains.

"Somebody has to look at me," she repeated with determination. "And if nobody will, then I'll do it myself." And she did just that.

It was days before anyone noticed her absence from the royal table. Footmen and ladies-in-waiting tend to find only those things important that the king and queen find important, and what the king and queen ignore is also ignored by the royal household. Once she was found, not a great deal changed. Princesses are accustomed to having their own way, and Esperanza was a true princess. She could not be persuaded to leave her room. She ate her food in front of the mirror and placed her bed under a mirror. Years passed, and she would have remained sitting in front of the mirror forever and a day, or even longer, if Prince Viereg had not arrived on the island with a gust of the north wind.

"Your daughter's beauty is praised throughout the high north," he said to the king. "I have come to ask for her hand in marriage."

"Oh, ah, my daughter," muttered the king, clearly distracted. "I'm really very busy at the moment. A new ship has to be fitted out, and I need to order a figurehead, and all manner of bothersome things. Go and ask my wife."

"I have come to ask for your daughter's hand in marriage," said the prince to the queen.

The queen had just had new closets delivered by the carpenter of Langstrand, the best furniture maker on the mainland, and she was busy with her ladies-in-waiting, hanging up all of her gowns and making a little more space for them.

"My daughter," muttered the queen, obviously agitated. "Her hand . . . it must be here somewhere, I think." And then she looked in dismay at all of the piles of clothes that still had to be tidied away.

And so the prince went looking for the king's daughter himself and found her in front of the mirror. Not a single word of exaggeration had been spoken of her beauty in the high north. But when the prince asked for her hand, she smiled sadly, shook her head, and kept gazing into the mirror.

"We have mirrors too," said the prince. "And in the

winter there's crystal-clear ice all over, and you can see yourself in it from head to toe."

But the king's daughter shook her head and rang for a lady-in-waiting to see the prince out. He went, but he returned the following day to repeat his offer of marriage.

This state of affairs continued for several months. The palace gatekeeper told a visiting traveler about the situation.

"What the king's daughter needs is a visit from Mee, the singer of sorrows," said the traveler. "He sings at funerals and after mining disasters, after floods and forest fires, wherever people have need of the consolation that is called mourning."

The gatekeeper was a good father and a wise man. He looked around to check that no one was eavesdropping, because it is always dangerous to speak ill of a king and queen. "The princess's parents have never looked after her," he whispered. "What she needs most is someone to cheer her up."

"Hmmm, someone to cheer her up," said the traveler, who had visited distant lands and seen many things. "I hear that there is also a merrymaker, a girl with an accordion and colorful clothes, who makes people laugh and dance and be full of good cheer."

"What the princess needs," said the gatekeeper, "is someone who can make her cry and then make her laugh."

"Yes," enthused the traveler. "I've been told that they belong together, the merrymaker and the singer of sorrows. They were born on the same day. It was the midday hour, and the bells began to ring as the two mothers bore their children, one screaming while the other never uttered a word. . . ."

"What is the name of this girl?" asked the gatekeeper. "And where can we find her?"

The traveler thought about this. "Mitou," he said after a while. "Mitou is her name, I believe. But I do not know where she is to be found. I think the best thing would be to track down Mee, the singer of sorrows. Perhaps she is with him. They appear to belong together one way or another. They were born on the same day, at the midday hour, when . . ."

"Yes," said the gatekeeper. "I know. Screaming mothers and ringing bells and so forth. Listen. There is an old footman at the palace who would do anything for the king's daughter. When she was a little girl, he played with her and talked to her and taught her how to read, and if anyone could have been a good father to her, he's the one. But unfortunately, you have only one mother and father."

The gatekeeper told the old footman about the singer of sorrows, the footman told Prince Viereg, and the prince asked the king's leave to send someone to search for Mee and Mitou.

And so it came to pass that the old footman was sent out in the golden coach and, together with two companions, he set sail and made his way to the mainland.

The Merrymaker

The lord of the manor was as old as Methuselah and as rich as Croesus. All of the farms for miles around belonged to him. The tenant farmers would bring half of the harvest to their lord, and the hunters who hunted in the forests would give half of each deer or boar to the castle's head cook — always the rear half, where the juiciest parts are to be found. This lord of the manor had a son, Grullo, who was dreadfully ugly, both inside and out, and who was also getting on in years. He was waiting for his father to die so that he could inherit all of his property.

The lord of the manor also had a much younger wife, who had never loved him. And as often happens with women who do not love their husbands, she absolutely adored her son Grullo. Even when he was just a little boy, she found no food tasty enough for him, and none of the children of his age were deemed worthy to play with him. And as often happens with boys who are put on a pedestal by their mothers and never told "no," Grullo grew into a cosseted man who took everything and gave nothing.

When he was young and his ugliness had not yet fully revealed itself, he had lost his heart to the stablemaster's daughter. He was prepared to give her everything, but his mother spoke to his father, and the lord of the manor dismissed the stablemaster and drove him and his family from the estate. Since then, Grullo had known only the love of poor women who work themselves into a sweat in dark backrooms, and the kisses of calculating farmers' daughters who turned a blind eye to his ugliness while ogling his gold.

When the lord of the manor finally died, at the age of one hundred, Grullo threw his mother out of the main part of the castle, rode into town, and knocked on the door of a marriage broker.

"I have exactly what you're looking for," said the cunning woman. "A young thing, pretty and blonde, fleet of foot, but with a heart that knows no haste. She has never yet kissed a man. She is as pure as snow, works like a horse, and is as fertile as a rabbit. She will surely give you an heir."

"Why would such a paragon of perfection want me?" asked Grullo. "I'm not handsome, I have no love to offer, and she does not sound to me like a woman who would be after my fortune."

The marriage broker laughed. "Her father has just died. He left behind a widow and seven children. Leatrice is the eldest, and she earns a little money by dancing in the tavern. But because she is virtuous and always goes home alone, she does not make enough money. Her mother and her little brothers and sisters are starving."

"That sounds good," said Grullo, and he rode at once to the tavern where Leatrice worked.

It was a place for rich folk, where the local gentlemen would spend their evenings. The mayor would drink to escape his mildewed bed and his scold of a wife; the judge would listen to the happy music and try to forget the blood-smeared necks of those he had sentenced to death; the doctor would puff away to rid himself of the stink of his patients; and the schoolmaster would seek refuge in the

rhythm of the dance from the endless monotony of frac-
tions and long division.

But, above all, they came to the tavern every evening to
watch Leatrice and to dance with her. She taught the
ungainly ones how to hold a lady; she patiently explained
the steps for the latest dance that was doing the rounds; she
knew all of the news about the local area; she listened to the
worries that the high-ranking gentlemen shared with her;
and she laughed merrily at their sweet talk.

During the day, when she took her few coins to go
shopping at the market for her mother and little brothers and sisters, she spoke to the wives of her regular
customers. She took the mayor's wife aside and pointed
out a discounted gown that might arouse her husband's
passion; she told the doctor's wife what the doctor's favorite dish was; and she asked the schoolmaster's wife, who
gave needlework lessons, about the progress of her own little
brothers and sisters. The townswomen trusted Leatrice
more than their own sisters, and with good reason. They
knew nowhere was safer for their husbands than the tavern,
except their own houses, and you can't really keep them
locked up at home.

So this was how things stood when Grullo called to pay his respects to Leatrice, and to put forward his proposition.

She was blonde and dainty and very beautiful, but when she gave him her response, her face was pale and her big blue eyes sparkled with something other than joy.

"I am to marry you and give you an heir, and you will provide for my mother and brothers and sisters, is that right? You will give me no love and you are not asking for love, and your riches will be for your descendants and not for me and my family."

"That's right," said Grullo.

"I'll have to ask my mother," said Leatrice.

Leatrice's mother and her little brothers and sisters begged her to accept Grullo's proposal.

"But he is ugly both inside and out," said Leatrice.

"Hunger and poverty are ugly too," said her mother.

"I'll accept the proposal," said Leatrice, "but I'll never come back here again."

"All right," said her mother. And her little brothers and sisters all shouted with joy.

The Merrymaker

Exactly nine months after the wedding, a baby girl was born. It happened in broad daylight, at the midday hour, and as Leatrice gave one last bloodcurdling scream and brought her child into the world, the bells began to ring and a flash of lightning rent the clear sky. It started to thunder and the rain poured down; the farmers had to cover their crops, and the lone traveler dismounted to seek shelter for his horse.

For four days, Leatrice hovered between life and death. On the fifth day, her mother-in-law came into the bedroom and took a good look at the newborn babe. The child had the blonde curls and the dainty little body of her mother, but old eyes like her father's.

"A hundred-hour child with hundred-year eyes," she said. "She shall be called Mitou." And she left.

When Leatrice had recovered, she got up from the bed, fed the child, saddled a horse, and rode into town. She put the money Grullo had given her into the bank and asked the bank manager, whom she knew from the tavern, to give her mother a fixed sum every month. Then she rode back to the castle at midday to feed the baby.

"I do not want you to leave the castle without my permission," said Grullo when she returned.

"I have married you and given you an heir," said Leatrice. "I cannot love a child that was conceived in loathing, but I will feed her and take care of her until she can stand on her own two feet. Then I will leave you. I cannot have any more children, the doctor has said, so there is no point in sharing your bed any longer." She moved into a wing of the castle opposite the rooms where her mother-in-law lived.

If Grullo had been a sensible man, he would have submitted to the inevitable. But his mother had spoiled him and taught him that he had a right to everything, and his wounded pride drove him to pursue Leatrice with complaints and demands. When the child was a year old and no longer drinking her mother's milk, Leatrice would leave her at home in the care of a nursemaid and ride out early in the morning. In the evening she would go dancing in the tavern as she had been accustomed to, because, as she said, she was "quite simply, good at it."

And when she got home, there were always two people waiting for her. One was her daughter, who soon crawled, then toddled and, later, ran to meet her, and the other was Grullo, who would block her path, cursing and ranting at her. Impatiently, Leatrice would push the child aside, but Grullo's fury seemed to infect her like a contagious disease, and before long she was outdoing him in curses and swear words and streams of abuse.

Little Mitou grew up in a world of ugly words. It's true that she had a kindhearted nursemaid, but it is the mother, with her sweet words and soothing voice, who instills in a child a love for listening and for talking.

Before Mitou could recognize the word "hug," or understand "lamb," her old-fashioned little head was full of "smug" and "sham." Before she learned to smile when someone said "sugarplum," her mind was packed with words like "ugly bum."

Mitou was quick to learn. When her nursemaid said, "Come and sit on my lap," she thought she'd said something about a "slap," so she would run off crying. She heard "You must be crazy!" when someone said "Look! A daisy!" and "I hope you die" instead of "Don't you cry."

Grullo and Leatrice had a wide range of terms of abuse, and they enjoyed making up new ones all the time, so it was not long before every sound and syllable in Mitou's little head had become infected. It was as though the words carried a deadly disease within themselves, as contagious as the Black Death. Before long, the little girl would cower as soon as anyone said anything at all, even if it was just the cook's boy asking what she wanted for her dinner.

By the time Mitou was three years old, she avoided all creatures with the power of speech. She played with the animals in the yard, she groomed the horses, she removed the burrs from the sheep's wool and the ticks from the dog's fur, and she fed the chickens and their chicks in the poultry pen. When it was cold, she would go to the attic, which ran across the length and breadth of the castle, and there she would play silent games with toy bears and old rags. She ignored the antique dolls that had been stored up there for as long as anyone could remember, because she didn't trust them to keep their pursed-up porcelain mouths shut.

Sometimes, to annoy Grullo, Leatrice would take the little girl along to the tavern. Then Mitou would sit on a high stool in the corner and, as long as no one spoke to her, she enjoyed the merriment, the aroma of food and drink, and the music. She watched her beautiful mother, who had finally stopped quarreling and was instead doing magnificent twirls on the dance floor. Mitou waved her little legs in the air and copied the movements her mother made.

When Mitou was four years old, she found a worn-out old accordion in the attic, the kind that children play or that an impoverished musician might use to earn a meager crust at fairs and village celebrations. She taught herself to play it, and made new tunes out of the music that she heard at the tavern. From then on, she and the accordion were inseparable, and when her mother and father were screaming curses at each other, she would play her accordion so loudly that she could no longer hear their yelling. All she could see was the twisted mouth of her mother making strange movements, and the red, flushed face of her father, and without any sound it all looked so funny that she would burst out laughing, because she was, by nature, a cheerful little girl.

She spent her first four years of school huddled up in the back row. She had to leave her accordion at home, and she tried to shut her ears to the infected words that the children and teachers bandied around. During her last two years of school, she received lessons from the schoolmaster, the same one who danced every evening in the tavern with her mother Leatrice. The schoolmaster loved Leatrice, and so he took an interest in the fate of her silent little daughter. By talking to her in a gentle and friendly way, day in and day out, and never threatening or punishing her, he managed to rob the infected words of some of their power.

The schoolmaster brought Mitou to the point where she would listen, at first just to him and his wife, who gave needlework lessons and was a sweet and friendly woman, and later to those children in her class who spoke calmly and did not use any terms of abuse. But Mitou herself did not say a word. In the morning, as she walked through the woods from the castle to the school, she would listen to the cheerful whistling of the birds and wish that she could sing out all of the worries of her heart, like a little bird herself.

When Mitou was twelve years old, Leatrice left the estate without saying good-bye. She took a room in the city, above the tavern. At least once a week, old Grullo would go to the tavern, and then they would call each other all the names under the sun in front of all of the other customers. At first, the landlord complained about these screaming matches, because he was afraid of losing customers. But Leatrice and Grullo were so gifted at swearing and ranting and cursing that they became famous throughout the entire region. When Grullo tied up his horse at the front door of the tavern, the news spread like wildfire, and the customers soon came flocking so as not to miss any of the sights and sounds of this spectacle. It was not unusual to spot an industrious clerk sitting here or there among the breathless audience, busily noting down all of the newly coined insults in order to sell them at the market to other couples who were battling each other and keen to expand their range of abusive vocabulary.

And so it happened that throughout the whole area on Saturday evening, when the exhausted men came home from work, looking forward to a long evening and a free day, their worn-out wives would be waiting for them with Leatrice's latest coarse terms of abuse, which were swiftly countered by Grullo's most recent base accusations. Never before had the long Saturday evening and the dull, empty Sunday been so full of variety and entertainment.

Meanwhile, Mitou had peace and quiet. But in the silence that had fallen upon the castle with the departure of her mother, she became so bored that she almost missed the quarrels. She played with the animals up in the attic; once a week she visited her mother in the town; and the rest of the time she practiced on her accordion. And one day, when the persistent cook's boy asked her what she wanted for dinner that evening, she played a happy tune to bolster her courage and said: "Chicken with applesauce."

Her own voice startled her, but the cook's boy smiled and brought her a large piece of roast chicken with fresh applesauce that evening.

And that is how Mitou learned to talk to people, to the accompaniment of the accordion, which protected her from the black word-plague. And everywhere she went and played her merry tunes, people would start singing and dancing, and they would forget all of their worries for a little while.

When Mitou was fourteen years old and had been out of school for two years, she started to wish more and more frequently that she could leave the estate and lead her own life, but she did not know how she might earn her daily bread.

It was at this time that the stories about Mee, the singer of sorrows, reached the small town in the distant forests of the east where Mitou lived. The men told each other in the tavern about the silent boy with the sad, dark eyes, who never smiled and who was able to get to the bottom of people's grief and sing it all out.

"He knows right away what the problem is," they said to one another in excited tones. "And then he starts singing about it and all of your sadness and pain are absorbed into his songs of sorrow. You wouldn't believe your eyes or ears."

Others told stories about his deaf-mute parents and his mysterious birth and the storm that had suddenly broken out in a clear sky.

"It was the midday hour," they said, "and the bells began to ring as his mother gave birth to the child without uttering a single word. Suddenly a flash of lightning rent the sky, and it began to thunder and to pour with rain, and the farmers had to cover their crops, the lone traveler had to crawl beneath his horse for shelter, and the fishermen out at sea had to lower their sails."

"That was the same moment my daughter was born," Leatrice would say then, and she would nod toward Mitou in her corner, because even though she could not love a child that had been conceived in loathing, she was not ill-disposed toward her.

Leatrice's words kept echoing around Mitou's head. So there was a silent boy, Mee, who had been born at the same moment as her birth, and who, according to the rumors, was traveling from west to east. If she were to travel toward him, she would be bound to find him, because his reputation preceded him and people for miles around would know where he was to be found.

So, one day, Mitou packed her knapsack, hung her accordion around her neck, and set off on her journey. She was dreaming of the day when she and Mee would travel the world together, and he would console people with his songs of sorrow and she would make them dance and sing. He was a silent boy; she had taken good note of that fact. But Mitou was not afraid of silence.

She slept in haystacks and stables, and ate what she found on the way and what people gave her. Everywhere she went, at markets and in town squares, in poor hamlets and wealthy villages, she would look for a large stone or well or some other raised platform upon which to stand, because she was only small, and then she would start to play and to sing.

It never took long for the villagers to start arriving in droves. The farmers would leave their fields and the washerwomen would leave their tubs, the schoolteacher would run out of the classroom with all of the children, and the miller would forget to take off his dusty white apron before dashing out with his wife and his servants to make merry. Because when Mitou started playing, everyone danced. The men would whirl their wives around, the lads and lasses would join hands and reel across the village square or meadow, and the little children would jump up and down to the tune of the accordion.

"Stay the night here with us, at the inn," the villagers would say when she had finished playing. "We'll give you a delicious meal and a soft bed filled with down and made with starched sheets."

But Mitou knew that the meals would be accompanied by words, as are most activities involving people. There would be tattling and teasing, whispering and wheedling, and finally, when the jugs were empty and the stomachs were full, there would be tormenting and cursing, and the black word-plague would take hold of Mitou and never let her go.

And so all she asked for was something to eat on her journey and, in return for her performance, a keepsake — a ribbon, or a trinket, a flowery jacket, a colored skirt, or a hat. She always left before daybreak, and the children of the village or hamlet would walk along with her for miles and beg her for one last happy song.

And so it came that Mitou's name and fame were just as widespread in the east as Mee's name and fame were in the west, and in the middle of the country it would have been impossible to say which of the two had garnered more renown.

And yet Mee had never heard the name of Mitou. Because, after all, people at funerals and memorial services have other things on their minds than rumors about a peculiar creature with a young body and old eyes, the finest merrymaker in the land.

The Army Captain

It was a glorious day. Mee was heading east, over the flat land that came after the mountains and the marshes. The roads were wide there, with a lot of traffic, and carts loaded high with goods being transported from the harbors to the countryside, and from the countryside to the harbors. Sometimes Mee would ride a short way on a cart, lying comfortably on bales of wool, or bouncing painfully among copper kettles and other household goods. Usually, however, he preferred to walk. When his legs were hurting from a long journey, when he had blisters on his feet and his stomach was rumbling with hunger, he felt good. *I have no right to an easy life,* he would say to himself. *A man who cannot make his own mother happy does not deserve to enjoy himself.*

Mee heard the thud of footsteps and glanced idly at a group of soldiers who were marching along two by two, in perfect step. They must have had a few days' marching behind them, as their uniforms and boots were dusty and their faces and hands were covered in sweat. Mugs, knives, and chunks of gray bread hung from their knapsacks.

The soldiers were not singing. Their faces were set and their eyes were focused on the road ahead, not on the glorious view and the green fields around them.

"Company, halt!" called the captain.

The soldiers came to an immediate stop. They looked straight ahead.

"Boy!" called the captain.

Mee was startled to hear the familiar name by which his parents had always addressed him and, without thinking, he started to make hand signs. *Boy, that's me,* said Mee softly, with the language of his hands.

"You there!" shouted the captain.

Mee gave him a sad smile.

"Hey, you!" called the captain. "We're looking for the singer of sorrows!"

"That's me," mumbled Mee.

"Yes, that's his name, Mee!" bawled the captain. "Do you know where we can find him?"

Mee placed one hand on his chest. "I am Mee, the singer of sorrows," he said.

The jaws of the soldiers dropped as one. "Mee!" came the cries from fifty mouths.

The captain marched stiffly over to Mee and saluted. "We're on our way to a military funeral," he said. "You would be doing us a great service if you would accompany us and sing a song of sorrow for our lieutenant with the flute, who fought for his fatherland and is now dead. Soldiers from all over the country are on their way to pay him their final respects. The army has been plunged into mourning."

Mee nodded. In the silence that followed the captain's words, a clattering noise could be heard. Mee looked over his shoulder and saw, in the distance, a glittering coach approaching. The coachman was waving his whip.

"Come along!" called the captain.

Mee hesitated. At that moment, a golden wheel became detached from the coach and rolled into the roadside. The coach rattled to a halt and tipped over to one side. Mee ran back to offer help, but farmhands came running from every direction and reached it first.

"Come along!" called the captain again. He pulled Mee with him.

The soldiers' spirits had noticeably improved. Now that they had Mee with them, their grief seemed easier to bear. They marched quickly onwards and soon reached the church where the lieutenant was laid out in his full regalia. The soldiers looked in awe at his uniform, which was covered with medals.

Mee looked at the face of the dead man, whose eyes were closed, and slowly his head filled with thoughts about the lieutenant's life and death.

At the front of the church, just before the altar, were velvet-covered chairs, upon which generals, majors, and other high-ranking officers had comfortably installed themselves. The soldiers, who had a three-day march behind them and still felt it in their legs, had to find somewhere to stand and then remain on their feet throughout the whole service.

The band played a funeral march. Mee went and stood beside the bier and started singing. The brass players lowered their instruments, and the drummer laid down his drumsticks, because the key in which Mee sang did not belong to any system of sounds that they knew, and they had no way of grasping the rhythm of his semi-comprehensible words.

Mee had only just started singing when he suddenly fell silent — maybe even in the middle of a sentence, but it was hard to say. From the rafters of the church came the piercing sound of a flute, soft at first, but becoming louder; the haunting, trilling notes of a wooden flute, of the kind that country boys cut from willow branches with a sharp pocketknife, the sort of flute that develops its own tone with the passing of the years. And for all of the soldiers who had ever heard it, this flute, echoing invisibly through the church, was, quite unmistakably, the willow flute of the dead lieutenant.

Only when the flute had fallen silent did Mee continue his song of sorrow.

The Lieutenant with the Flute

The wool-dyer had seven sons. Ranko was the youngest and the smartest. After his birth, the wool-dyer's wife lay down upon her bed, with the shutters closed, and never got up again.

"I have a headache," she whispered to the wool-dyer when he came to ask her what was wrong. "I have a headache, or the headache has me, and stop shouting like that."

Little Ranko spent the first years of his life in an ink-dark room, where he drank his mother's milk to the sweet accompaniment of her lamentations. As it is difficult to play in the dark, he amused himself by making little sounds, quiet sounds that did not wake his mother from her drowsing. He learned the difference between knocking on wood, tapping on metal, and thumping on cloth, and between his feeds and his changes he fumbled his way around the bedroom like a blind mole in a dark tunnel.

Once Ranko could walk and had found the way outside all by himself, he looked at the world, painfully blinking and full of bewilderment.

The world was light. Sunlight glimmered on the leaves of the big willow tree by the well, on the beaks of the ducks in the pond, on the locks of the double barn doors, and in the eyes of his six silent brothers, who had come running when one of them saw the little boy standing in the doorway.

The world was full of colors. The thatched roof of the barn was yellow, the smocks of the boys were blue, and skeins of red wool hung drying all over the yard.

The world did not smell of his mother's milk. The blossom on the apple trees had the scent of nectar, the washed wool drying on the racks smelled of green soap, the cow parsley gave off a sweetish odor, and over everything hung the pungent smell of madder dye coming from the tub of red wool.

The world made noise. The wind whistled in the leaves of the trees, the ducks quacked, the birds sang, a cow lowed in the distance, and the wheels of a cart rattled on the road beside the yard.

The world was in motion. There were chickens running about the yard, birds flying back and forth to their nests in the trees, clouds scudding across the sky, and before long the motionless brothers started to fidget with their hands and shuffle with their feet. Finally, they stepped forward as one and embraced their brother, whom they had never before seen by daylight.

In short, the world was full of life.

But even then there was no chance to play. The wool-dyer had lost his wife as a worker, and the boys had to help out in the dye house, and that included the seventh son, even though he was barely old enough to walk. They made the red wool that the local women used to weave their shawls, and all of the skeins had to be exactly the same shade of red. The oldest and strongest boys carried endless pails of water from the well to the rinsing basins; the youngest stirred the dye tub with long wooden sticks; and Ranko chased away the chickens and the ducks when they tried to land on the freshly washed and dyed wool with their dirty feet.

One day, when he was about six, he was running after a wayward rooster and he fell into the duckweed-covered pond. No one heard the boy cry out. He sank to the bottom and became entangled in the water plants. He opened his eyes to see a familiar inky blackness, which calmed him. The memory of the scent of his mother's milk filled his lungs. His foot slipped free of the plants, and he floated to the surface.

When the wool-dyer and his sons realized that Ranko had disappeared, they ran to the pond in a terrible fright, and saw Ranko surfacing among the duckweed. He was splashing around with his arms and legs and just managing to keep afloat. The wool-dyer pulled him to the side and threw him into the air with his strong arms, which were red from the madder dye, and because the boys were so wild with excitement and all wanted a turn, it did not take long before the grass beside the pond was covered with a red tangle of boys, all romping and rolling.

It was a Saturday and there was no more work that day. The wool-dyer cooked a meal, sat in silence beside the bed of his suffering wife for a while, and then left for the village inn to drown his sorrows and to toast his joy after his little lad's close escape.

As everyone knows, the life of a wool-dyer is full of snags and tangles. The number of dye works in foreign countries was increasing, as taxes there were lower and workers were cheaper; this meant the price of the rare dye had doubled. The fine wool that came from overseas was captured by pirates, so the dyer had to obtain wool from the northern isles, which was worse in quality, but higher in price.

In the old days, thought the wool-dyer gloomily as he sat with a glass of brandy, he had poured out all of his sorrows and his joy during his nightly embraces in the arms of his wife. With moans and sighs and stammered words, he would share with her all of his worries. "Let out your sorrows," she would whisper soothingly. "Cry on my shoulder. Just let it all flow." Then, once a year, she would let out all of the sorrows he had cried upon her shoulder, and a new little wool-dyer would see the light of day. But for the past few years he had had no one with whom to share his joy and his sorrows.

Sooner or later, something had to give, and on that very Saturday the pent-up worries of the wool-dyer forced their way out in a violent flood of rage that no one could stem.

Swearing and cursing, he rode home, and he gave a sound beating to the first son to cross his path, with his belt and with the stirring stick. The wool-dyer thrashed the boy with all the strength of his red arms, which could never be washed completely clean of the madder dye. He could find no other way to lighten his heart.

If a man wants to let out his emotions, a woman's shoulder is perfectly suited to the task. Children's bodies, however, are not. The boy screamed with terror and pain, and his six brothers came out and watched their raging father, paralyzed with fear. When his anger had cooled, the wool-dyer stumbled inside to sleep it off. Relieved by the fit of fury, he went back to work on Monday, but after that he would increasingly often fly into a rage and beat his sons, because anger, when it is released in the wrong way, merely creates new anger.

Whichever of his sons he took it out on, it was never Ranko, his youngest boy. Ranko was a born escape artist. All he needed to hide himself was a roof beam; he'd just stretch out on it and wait for the storm to blow over. Sometimes, if it hadn't rained for a long time, he'd scramble into the rain barrel; on other occasions, he'd climb up among the dense branches of the willow tree.

Ranko had never forgotten the day when he had come outside for the first time and stood before his six bigger brothers, and there was no one in the world that he loved more than them. So he created hiding places for all six of them, in nooks and crannies in the house and the barn, in the yard and the overgrown vegetable garden. He carved a flute for himself from the willow tree, and when he saw his father coming home, reeling and ranting, he would blow on his flute. And all of the boys would run for shelter.

The wool-dyer stood no chance against his seven sons. It was always Ranko who would run out to meet him. "Father! Father!" he would cry joyfully, in the hope that the wool-dyer's anger would turn into happiness. As soon as the boy saw that this change had not occurred, he would turn around, cry out "Catch me if you can!" and take to his heels. If it hadn't been so sad, it would have been a funny sight, the speedy little lad in front, followed by the heavy man, swaying and swearing, running after him, with his bloodred arms and a stirring stick he had picked up along the way to serve as a cudgel. As he ran, Ranko would keep stopping for a second to give all of his brothers time to find a safe spot. And then the boy would suddenly disappear, as though he had gone up in smoke, and the wool-dyer would stand there, staring around with his bloodshot eyes and foaming mouth, and a bewildered expression on his face. After an hour of yelling and searching, he usually collapsed to sleep it off, and then Ranko, who had never left the yard, would blow on his willow flute to announce that the coast was clear.

Nature created the young of the human species weak and small. The child is helpless and at the mercy of the powerful hands and feet of its procreator. But so as to compensate a little, people are made to be fertile, so that parents are soon outnumbered by their offspring.

It was not long before the oldest son equaled his father in strength and size. One evening the wool-dyer came home drunk and found seven sons waiting for him, the oldest at the front. They did not run away. They blocked his path and looked at him, and when the wool-dyer raised a shaking fist, the boy at the front lifted his fist as well. It was a strong, rough hand, which could never be washed completely clean of the madder, and it did not shake.

"You are our father," said the young man. "You take care of our mother and you work hard to give us food. We shall allow you to pass." They went and stood at the side of the road and the wool-dyer staggered past. His reign of cruelty was over for good.

The boys all left home as soon as they were old enough to make their own ways. Ranko enlisted in the army. There too he distinguished himself through his courage and his skill, and before long he achieved the rank of lieutenant. He was given the nickname of "flutenant" by the soldiers in his section, because he always kept his willow flute close at hand.

Soon after Ranko's promotion to lieutenant, disorderly bands of marauding mercenaries invaded the land from the south. The general of the army in Ranko's land was a real bully, and he liked nothing better than making other men fight. He sent all five of his captains and their companies to the south with orders to annihilate the enemy. When Ranko's superior officer fell and broke his leg, Ranko took charge of the fifth company.

But, oh dear, when a small country wants to go to war against a large realm, it's like a chick fighting a rooster. As soon as the king from the south heard that his soldiers, even if they were only marauding mercenaries, had been attacked, he sent all of his troops to the north.

Ranko and his men were encamped in a small village whose inhabitants had fled. One day his orderly came to report. He saluted Ranko and said: "A deserter from the third company has reached our village, lieutenant." In front of the church, by the village pump, lay a heavily wounded soldier. He had only one arm and one-and-a-half legs, and the amount of blood soaking his uniform made it impossible to see what other injuries he might have. His face was as pale as marble, and his eyes were closed tight.

"Execute him, lieutenant?" asked the second lieutenant, who was a stickler for the rules and had high aspirations for himself.

"Waste of a bullet," said Ranko curtly.

"That's true," grinned the second lieutenant. "Anything's wasted on a cowardly deserter like that."

That was not what Ranko meant. The poor soldier was already close to death. Ranko knelt down beside him.

"All of them slaughtered," mumbled the dying soldier. "Four of our companies." Then he died.

The orderly came running over. "Report from the lookout," he panted. "Enemy troops approaching."

In the distance, the rumble of rattling wheels could be heard and the cheers of a victorious army returning home.

"Take cover," said Ranko. "Everyone."

"That's treason," said the second lieutenant. "Our orders are to defend ourselves to the last man."

"Take cover!" shouted Ranko. The orderly ran off to inform the soldiers.

"We're going to lie in ambush," Ranko told his subordinate. "When I blow on my flute, and not a second before, you all come out, and then you can fight to the last man."

Satisfied, the second lieutenant went to take cover.

Ranko stayed in the village square until the scouts from the southern army entered the village. Then he suddenly disappeared, as though he had gone up in smoke. When Ranko finally blew on his flute and his men appeared with their rifles at the ready, a cloud of dust to the south, near the border, was all that could be seen of the departing enemy army.

Ranko and his men headed back north and arrived safely at headquarters, where the second lieutenant reported Ranko for high treason, and he was sentenced to death.

"You may have one last word," said the general, who was presiding over the court-martial.

"The world is full of life," Ranko said with a smile.

"Execute him!" barked the general, who was in a bad mood because he had lost the war, and a few thousand men besides.

Ranko was blindfolded with a black cloth and made to stand against the wall of the barracks. As all of the other soldiers in the army had been killed, his own unit was ordered to shoot him.

It was a beautiful, warm day. The sun was shining, but for Ranko the world had gone dark. He thought about the first years of his life in the darkened bedroom, and the scent of his mother's milk entered his nostrils. Calmly, he breathed in and out and smiled.

The news that the savior of the fifth company was to be executed had quickly spread throughout the land. As Ranko's men took aim with tears in their eyes, a crowd of silent men, women, and children thronged onto the parade ground. No guard had stopped them at the gate; all of the guards were dead. The crowd of townsfolk stood in silence before Ranko, and hundreds of eyes watched the soldiers.

As one man, the soldiers gave a half turn and aimed at the general, who, seated high on his horse and decorated with all of his medals, had come to enjoy the execution.

The general turned his horse around and dug in his spurs. He never returned to the barracks. Rumor has it that he offered his services to the army from the south, and was given an important position, as though the notion of "high treason" exists only for the lower ranks.

Ranko's honor was restored. For some time, there was little reason to fight. Peace had been made with the kingdom to the south.

But on either side of the country, there were two larger realms, and those two realms started to wage war upon each other. The poor little country in the middle was by turns trampled underfoot by the soldiers from the neighboring country to the left and then by the one to the right. The armies from the left-hand country wrecked and plundered the villages as they passed through, and also murdered as many of the villagers as possible, because those who have once tasted blood will always thirst for it. Resistance was useless. The armies were simply too powerful. And by the time the surviving villagers had built their houses again and replowed their fields, the fortunes of war would have turned and the armies of the right-hand country would pass through the land, pillaging and murdering.

Only in the mountain villages did the people escape this terrible fate. When they saw the soldiers approaching in the distance, they loaded their possessions onto goats and donkeys and hid in the caves and tunnels above the tree line, where inexperienced climbers did not dare to venture. If a looting army climbed up the mountain to find it a wasted effort, the soldiers would set the empty houses on fire in their anger, but on their next raid, they would simply pass over the mountain villages.

It was from this safe hiding place that Lieutenant Ranko assumed responsibility for the campaign of concealment, which was the people's best form of defense. With his unit of personally trained Hiders, he traveled all over the land and managed to create hiding places in even the flattest and most inhospitable of landscapes. Every soldier knows that you have to stab haystacks with a bayonet or a pitchfork to find out if somebody is hiding there, and then, in time-honored fashion, you have to set the haystack on fire. But neither the soldiers of the left-hand army nor those of the right-hand army came up with the idea that the secret hiding place might not be in the haystack, but in the ground beneath it. Ranko and his Hiders left behind a tightly knit network of hiding places in hollow oaks, double-bottomed feeding troughs, tree houses, and underground tunnels.

Sometimes, as they were making a hiding place, they were threatened by the approach of a stray band of looters. "Hiders, take cover," Ranko would say. He himself always remained in the middle of the village square until the last of his men and the villagers, including the pregnant women, small children, and hobbling graybeards, had hidden themselves away with their possessions. At the very last moment, as the first looters were entering the village, he would mysteriously disappear from sight. And when the whole village had been burned to the ground and no house was left standing, when even the cellars had been searched and destroyed and the soldiers had slunk away without any spoils, he would suddenly reappear in the middle of the village square, playing a rippling melody on his willow flute as a sign that the coast was clear.

When the armies from the left and the right could no longer find anything to feed themselves with as they passed through the country in the middle, the war between the two countries came to a natural end. The king of the left-hand country married the princess of the country in the middle, and the country by the coast then became part of the fatherland, or the other way around. Years later, the country on the right also became part of the same realm. Ranko had in the meantime been promoted to captain, but all of the soldiers still knew him as the "flutenant."

As an old man, Ranko felt his end approaching, and he left for the house where he had first seen the light of day in a darkened bedroom. The house was deserted and dilapidated. The tubs in the yard were red from the dried-in wool dye, and they reminded Ranko of the madder-red arms of his hard-handed father.

"A Hider does not fight death, a Hider dies in hiding," Ranko said out loud. He gave a salute, got undressed, as he had done hundreds of times before, hid his clothes, and then climbed down the well in the yard.

As he disappeared beneath the water, he placed his fingers on the holes of his willow flute, pushed the flute through the surface of the water, and breathed slowly in and out, as he had done hundreds of times before when he had had to hide from his father and his enemy. Peacefully, he blew out his final breath in his wet hiding place, in the inky darkness of the first years of his life.

And that is how the villagers found him, floating at the bottom of the well, the walls echoing with the haunting notes of a flute — soft at first, but becoming louder, which no one could explain.

The Farrier

Mee kept on heading east. As long as he was leaving the coast behind him he felt safe. It was a beautiful spring day, but Mee did not see that. He climbed up and down a high hill and had almost reached the bottom when he heard a loud clattering behind him. He stopped walking and looked back.

At the top of the hill appeared a glittering carriage, drawn by two Lipizzaners. *It's as though I'm being followed*, thought Mee, but he didn't care. When he was not doing his work and was wrapped up in the life story of a person who had died, nothing in the world could touch him. The greatest sorrow on this earth pales beside grief for a dead mother. Mee carried on walking.

Suddenly his knees gave way and he fell. His leg was bleeding. A horseshoe had fallen from one of the horses' hooves and rolled down the hill, where it hit Mee hard in the back of his knee. At the top of the hill, the glittering coach had now come to a halt.

A horse and cart came out of a side road. The driver stopped and knelt down beside Mee. He examined the wound, which was not deep, and helped Mee to his feet.

"Where are you heading, lad?" he asked. Mee pointed eastwards.

"Why don't you ride along with me?" said the driver. "But first you have to tell me whether you know where the singer of sorrows is. I'm looking for him."

Mee placed one hand on his chest. "That's me. Mee," he said. "The singer of sorrows. How can I be of service?"

The driver fell to his knees. "Mee," he implored, "everything in my village is going to the dogs. The women are no longer cooking and washing, the farmers are not mowing and threshing, the schoolteacher is not teaching the little children how to do their sums, and the children are not playing outside. The farrier's wife, who was no one's woman but her own, climbed onto a saddle rack and hanged herself with the reins of a bridle."

Mee sighed. "I'll come with you," he said.

The Farrier

It was a long journey. Fortunately, the driver had brought food with him, and he laid jute sacks on the floor of the cart, so Mee could make himself comfortable and wanted for nothing.

It was springtime. The fields were pale green with new shoots of growth, and sturdy little lambs and young goats frolicked in meadows full of poppies and cornflowers. The trees were coming into bud, and wild anemones and wood violets blossomed in their shade.

Mee looked neither left nor right. He could see only a familiar face before him with dark, slanting eyes and beloved, nimble hands.

Mee had never encountered a faster horse than the gelding that was pulling their cart. Before he knew it, they had reached the farrier's village. The farrier made shoes for all of the horses in the area and took care of their hooves. He also kept his own horses — not the heavy cream-colored nags with feathered legs that help farmers with their work, but lean, skittish thoroughbreds. As the cart entered the village, Mee saw them all grazing together in small groups, with the exception of two black Arabians prancing around at opposite ends of their own fenced-off paddock.

Mee leapt down from the cart, said good-bye to the driver, and made his way to the farrier's workshop. He saw nobody working, and even the chickens and goats in the yards were perfectly still. Only the pigs were still rooting away in the mud.

The only person in the whole village who was working was the farrier himself. He had placed the hoof of a huge carthorse on the foot stand and was nailing a shoe onto it.

"The horse-master's daughter would have wanted it this way," he said to Mee when he saw him standing beside him.

"The horse-master's daughter?" asked Mee.

The farrier did not look up from his work. "Folicia always said, 'If you don't want to call me by my name, then you can just call me the horse-master's daughter.' After we married, they called her 'the farrier's wife,' but she was no one's woman but her own."

He banged in the final nail, called a man to take away the horse, and led the way into the house beside the workshop.

The horse-master's daughter was laid out in the front

room. She had black hair, as black as the Arabians outside in the paddock, and it was loose around her tanned face. She was wearing a green riding habit and beside her lay a gleaming leather whip.

"She never used it," said the farrier, shedding silent tears at the sight of his dead wife. "She had a natural mastery of horses."

People came flocking from every direction. The women who had come to the house of mourning for the funeral preparations were unable to do anything because of their helpless sorrow, so they sat down around the bier; the farmhands and maids stood around it, and the mourners from the village and beyond, who had heard about the arrival of the singer of sorrows, laid their clogs by the door and silently entered the front room in stocking feet.

When Mee looked for the first time at the farrier's wife, who was no one's woman but her own, he felt no sorrow in her, but a great, effervescent love of life, which he had no idea how to handle.

The farrier sat waiting patiently for Mee to start singing. Mee looked around at the mourners, who had all pinned their hopes on him. He looked for a second time at the farrier's wife, who was no one's woman but her own. And this time he was filled with the overwhelming sadness that comes about when a great, effervescent love of life is transformed into a burning desire for death. He took a deep breath and began to sing.

The Horse-Master's Daughter

Growing up, she ran wild, with no mother. Because the horse-master's wife — who, just like her daughter later, was no one's woman but her own — took to her heels when the child Folicia was three years old.

Folicia could ride a horse before she could walk. Her father, the horse-master, bought her a pony, but she would ask the stable boy to lift her up onto the old mare, and then she would ride around, first walking, later at a trot and at a gallop. Because she couldn't get down from the horse by herself, she took her afternoon naps on the broad back of the mare, who carried on walking and rocked her to sleep.

The child was a burden to none. She was as obedient as a thoroughbred stallion that has always been treated well, and when the horse-master took her along on his trips around the area, she would quietly sit waiting for him in the cart until he had finished his work.

The local farmers and horse breeders would call for her father's help when they were training a stubborn carthorse or breaking in a thoroughbred foal. He also examined pregnant mares and helped when it was time for them to give birth. There was a veterinary surgeon in the area, but he had studied in the city. Folicia's grandfather had been a horse-master, as had his father and grandfather, and the knowledge of the profession had been passed down from generation to generation in such a way that it almost seemed hereditary.

Still, Folicia never went with her father into the barns or paddocks that he visited. Even as a young girl, she hated her father's job. She would cower in the cart when she heard a foaling mare whinny out in pain; she hated the cracks of the whip as the horses ran around the track in the training school.

But what horrified her most was the breaking-in of foals. However tame they may seem, horses are born wild. Folicia had once watched as her father had broken one of their own horses to his will. He started with a thin rope, which he placed around the foal's neck. Weeks went by before the young animal learned to put up with this indignity. Getting the horse accustomed to a saddle took an even longer time. Even the lightest, softest lace handkerchief placed upon its back was instantly thrown off by the fiery foal. A great many cracks of the whip and large amounts of carrot and candy were necessary before the wild young horse became a willing mount.

Folicia rode without saddle, reins, or bit, and she swore to herself that when she was older she would not have her horses shod either. Horseshoes were not needed in the soft pastures and in the forests, and she had no cause to ride on the road to the village and the city.

At school Folicia was a quiet and hardworking child. She was eager to learn and quick to obey if the teacher was fair and did not shout at her. One time a schoolmaster had hit her, for something she had not done, and then she had kicked backwards with her foot and given him such a blow that it broke his kneecap. The horse-master was an important man in the area, so the incident had no consequences for Folicia. After the teacher had apologized to her, she simply returned to school.

By the time she reached sixteen, Folicia was the most beautiful and desirable woman for miles around. As she rode through the forests with her long black hair flying out behind her, the young woodcutters would drive their axes into the tree trunks to watch her ride past. The farmers' sons in the fields would bring their draft horses to a halt and climb up on their hay carts so that they could see her for as long as possible. But Folicia saved all of her attention for horses.

The only man with any chance of winning her heart was the young farrier. He was short and thickset, but he had the athletic build of a thoroughbred, with muscular arms and legs, large hands and feet, and a straight back. He courted Folicia with the same patience and controlled force with which he shod his horses.

He proposed to her regularly, every time there was a full moon. He would wait until she came out for her evening ride, then he would let her ride away, and spur on his horse to follow her. In the forest was a clearing where Folicia would always dismount. A stream babbled through the clearing and Folicia would allow her horse to drink while she sat and rested under a tree. That was the place where the farrier always asked for her hand.

"I'll not allow anyone to hammer shoes onto me," Folicia would say. "The yoke of marriage does not bring happiness. I learned that at school." And she would laugh, because she was well aware that the farrier was a handsome young man.

She saw more of him than was wise. One day she rode to his workshop, then tapped him on the shoulder because he could not hear her for the banging of his hammer, and said: "I'm carrying your child."

"That's wonderful," said the farrier. "When shall we get married?"

"Whenever you want," said Folicia. She got back on the horse and galloped away.

"You mustn't ride that fast in your condition!" cried the farrier, but she was already too far away to hear him.

Whether it was because of her wild riding or not, seven days after the wedding Folicia lost the unborn child. It happened in the same clearing in the forest where the child had been conceived, and when it was all over, Folicia washed herself in the stream and rode back to the workshop.

"The child is gone," she said to the farrier.

"That's not good," said the farrier. "When you've recovered, we'll make a new one."

75

Folicia shook her head.

"Listen to me, my woman," said the farrier with controlled force.

"I am no one's woman but my own," said Folicia, "and anyone who doesn't want to call me by my name can just call me the horse-master's daughter."

Six times, by the light of the full moon, the farrier followed his wife to the clearing in the forest and begged her to love him. And six times Folicia got to her feet, jumped onto her horse, and galloped away.

The seventh time, the moon was brighter than ever. The clearing in the forest was bathed in light. Folicia waited for the farrier. He was late. When she heard the hooves on the soft forest floor, it sounded as though the horse had eight legs.

"I have brought a present for you," said the farrier. It was the most beautiful Arabian mare that Folicia or anyone else had ever seen. The moon was reflected in her gleaming black coat. She had big, dark eyes and silky soft ears. Her haunches and thighs were bundles of muscle, wrapped in velvet.

"She's a valuable horse," said the farrier. "I bought her

from a Gypsy king, and he brought her over from Arabia himself. She will not endure a saddle, bit, or reins, and that is why I bought her for you."

"Thank you," said Folicia.

"If we don't have to save our money to feed and clothe children," said the farrier a little sadly, "then we can afford expensive horses. But I want you to love me."

"All right," said Folicia. "We've waited long enough."

The Arabian mare became Folicia's favorite horse. She no longer wanted to ride any other horse, and she spent entire days combing its coat and tending to it.

"We have to find a stallion," she said to the farrier. "I can't wait to see foals from my mare."

"We can afford an expensive stallion," said the farrier quietly, "now that we don't have to spend our money on feeding and clothing children." He waited until the Gypsy king and his people were nearby and bought an Arabian thoroughbred.

The first foal that was born was the most beautiful little stallion that Folicia or anyone else had ever seen. He resembled his father and mother equally, both in appearance and temperament, because the foal, which was called

Number One, would not be tamed. You could tempt him to come to you with a carrot or a piece of candy, and you could touch him and rub his soft nose. But he would not endure a lace handkerchief on his back, nor a stick in his mouth to accustom him to the bit, nor a thread of wool around his neck. The farrier sold the animal as a breeding stallion.

Number Two was a mare. She was as wild as her father and mother. You could call her to you with a carrot or a piece of candy, but she would endure no touching, and certainly not a cambric handkerchief upon her back, nor a twig in her mouth, nor a thread of cotton around her neck. When Number Two was old enough to be ridden, Folicia carefully attempted to climb onto her back, but after a few weeks she gave up. The farrier sold the animal as a broodmare.

Number Three was another mare. She was as beautiful and wild as her brother and sister. She stayed close to her mother in the paddock, and you could not call her to you or tempt her with a carrot or a piece of candy, and you could certainly not touch her and stroke her nose, let alone place a feather on her back, stick a piece of straw in her mouth, or tie a silken thread around her neck.

Still, Folicia would stand for hours beside the paddock, watching her Arabians run. Number Three would gallop up to the fence, tossing her head and enjoying the admiration, then shy away at the last moment.

"Nobody wants to buy a foal from us now," said the farrier to Folicia. "Our horses are cursed because they belonged to a Gypsy and come from Arabia. That's what people are saying."

"We can just let her run about in the paddock," said Folicia. "There's enough space."

The farrier went pale. "It is true," he said, "that I can afford to keep a useless horse, given that I don't have to save my money to feed and clothe my children."

"Yes, that's true," said Folicia.

"But I have a reputation to protect as a farrier and a horse breeder," said the farrier. "When I go into town, people laugh at me because my wife would rather raise horses than children. What do you think they will say when they're worthless, useless horses to boot? Because things are going from bad to worse with these beasts."

"Animals," said Folicia. "Not beasts."

"You are a beast," said the farrier. He took Number Three into town and sold her to the horse butcher.

And when he came home that night he found his wife in the stable, hanging by the leather reins of a bridle, with a saddle rack kicked over beneath her dangling legs.

The Master Seaman

For three days and three nights, the horse-master's daughter was mourned by her family and friends. Even the pastures, fields, and stables were plunged into mourning. The slender, black Arabians neither whinnied nor ate; the huge carthorses left the hay uneaten in their mangers; ponies and mules and foals lay their little bodies down in the grass as though they were dead or sleeping.

On the morning of the fourth day, Mee moved on toward the east again. It was a glorious day, but at the midday hour, a flash of lightning rent the clear sky. Mee hurried on beneath the black clouds that were chasing across the heavens. The farmers covered their crops, and here and there a lone traveler sought shelter for himself and his horse.

It began to thunder and to pour with rain. Mee found a shed that was half full of hay. He climbed onto the hay, spread out his wet smock to dry, and took a hunk of bread and a piece of cheese from his knapsack.

He was about to sink his teeth into the bread when he was startled by a shrill noise. He looked around. Sitting against the opposite wall of the shed was a peculiar creature. She had the dainty little body of a young girl, but old eyes, and she was decked out in the most garishly bright colors that anyone could ever think of combining. She was playing a little tune that was so dreadfully cheerful and jolly that it made Mee's hair stand on end in distress.

"Please stop making that terrible noise!" said Mee.

"Nice to meet you," said the creature, without stopping playing. "My name's Mitou. What's yours?"

"Play a fiddle," grumbled Mee. "Play a flute, the bagpipes, a hurdy-gurdy, a drum, or a lute, but don't play one of those *things*." And he stuck his fingers in his ears.

"And you are Mee," said the peculiar creature, and she carried on playing regardless. "Because on a perfectly clear day the sky has started to flash with lightning and to pour with rain, the farmers have had to cover their crops, and lone travelers are seeking shelter for themselves and their horses."

Then she slid over to Mee, took a piece of his bread and cheese, and happily started to eat.

"That's my bread," said Mee. Then he realized that she was at least quiet when she was eating.

The storm passed over as they ate in silence. The sky cleared up and the fields began to steam in the watery sunshine. Mee packed up his things so as to be relieved of this unwelcome company as quickly as possible.

Mitou jumped down from the hay and followed after him. They stopped on the roadside to allow a horseman to pass, who was heading westward at full trot.

"Are you traveling westward as well?" Mee asked Mitou.

She gave him a radiant smile and nodded.

"I wish you a pleasant journey then," said Mee. "My path leads to the east." And with a sigh of relief, he went on his way.

He walked for some distance and came to a crossroads. A carriage was approaching along one of the side roads. It was drawn by two Lipizzaners, and its gilded woodwork flashed in the sun. As soon as the carriage came to a stop in front of Mee, three livery-clad footmen jumped out.

"Dear friend," they said to Mee. "Finally we have found you."

"Who have you found?" Mee asked suspiciously.

"You're Mee, the singer of sorrows, aren't you?" asked the oldest footman. "We met the farrier, galloping like a wild man through the fields on a black Arabian with no saddle, reins, or bit. He pointed us in the direction you went and told us what you looked like."

Mee gave a silent nod.

"The people of the island across the water need your help," pleaded the oldest footman. "The heiress to our throne is in a sorry plight. We ask you to accompany us to the harbor of Langstrand and sail on our ship to the island, to rescue the king's daughter from her sorrowful fate."

"I am not going to the coast," said Mee. "The scent of the dune roses reminds me of my mother. The sight of the waves causes me pain. Even the roar of the ocean stabs my heart."

"We have long been seeking you," said one of the other footmen. "But we had hoped to find you together with Mitou. . . ."

When Mee heard the name of Mitou, he glanced over

his shoulder. The footmen followed his gaze. In the distance, a small figure could be seen.

"No time to lose," said the eldest footman. He leaped into the coach. The other two picked up Mee, lifted him into the carriage, deposited him on a velvet seat, and kept a firm hold on him. The horses started to trot.

"Mitou!" cried the eldest footman when they came to a stop beside her.

Mitou looked at the gilded carriage with a crown on its side and the coat of arms of the island across the water. She saw Mee sitting between the footmen with a grumpy expression on his face. She nodded and got in silently.

"You see," she said when she was sitting opposite Mee, "where you go, I must go too." And she played a disgustingly cheerful little tune. "Because the sky flashed at midday on the day we were born, and the lone traveler . . ."

"Had to seek shelter with his horse," said Mee. "I know. So what?"

Mitou simply smiled. With irritation, Mee noticed that her old eyes were sparkling.

"The world dies in sorrow," said Mee. "If you saw what I see, the smile would die on your lips."

"The grass is green, the sky is blue, the birds are singing, and the flowers are blooming," was all Mitou replied.

"To the coast!" cried the old footman. The driver gave a click of his tongue and the Lipizzaners set off.

"What is the meaning of this?" asked Mee.

"You have to help us," said the old footman. "We have been traveling for weeks, searching for the two of you. We almost caught up with you, Mee, on a number of occasions, but each time we had some accident or other. Fate did not want us to find you before the two of you found each other."

"We haven't found each other," snapped Mee. "And what's so urgent that you feel you can drag me into this carriage against my will?"

The old footman sighed. "Since she was a young girl, Esperanza, our king's daughter, has sat before the mirror, looking at herself. She eats before the mirror, she sleeps beneath a mirror, she . . ." He blushed and said no more.

"Prince Viereg came to our island with a gust of the north wind," said the second footman, "to marry the king's daughter. He wants to take her back to his kingdom, but she cannot be dragged away from the mirror."

"I'm not the man for dragging people away from things," said Mee. "Look for a donkey driver or a prize fighter."

"Prince Viereg thinks that you can cheer up his beloved," said the third footman.

"I'm not the man for cheering people up," said Mee. "Ask Mitou whether she'll go with you." He threw a look of contempt at the girl sitting opposite him, who was taking great pleasure in absorbing the scents, colors, and sounds of the landscape. "Some people have no eye for misery," he added.

"The people of our island have pinned all of their hopes on the two of you," said the footmen. "If you, Mee, can see the soul of our princess, and understand why she is making her days so bitter, then perhaps you, Mitou, can give her back her love of life."

Mitou gave a cheerful nod, but Mee just shook his head. "My heart is tired," he said, "and full of gloomy thoughts. I cannot help the king's daughter."

"My son," said the eldest footman, "I am a man of advanced years. The worries of my life are carved in the wrinkles of my brow, the folds of my cheeks, and the lines around my mouth. Not so long ago, you were still a smooth-cheeked boy. It is not good for the young to bear the pains of the old. And so I shall tell you the tale of the king's daughter."

"As you wish," said Mee.

"There once lived a king and a queen who were always very busy," began the footman.

At the first words of the old man, Mee took a deep breath and his lungs filled with so much air that his chest seemed to open up and expand. It was not the sadness of the story that made his head swim and seemed to lift a weight from his shoulders. It was the soft voice of the wise old man. He seemed to be saying that one day Mee would be relieved of the arduous task of consoling the world.

Mee could feel his heart beating calmly in his chest. "All right, I'll go with you," he said when the old footman had finished speaking.

After a long journey, they rode over the bumpy cobbles of Langstrand to the harbor. Mitou breathed in the sea air with delight. She had never been to the coast before, and she raised her hand to shield her eyes so that she would be able to see the dunes and the ocean as soon as they came into view. When that time came, she gave a deep sigh and smiled to herself at so much beauty.

"We can board immediately," said the footmen. "Then we will set sail early tomorrow morning."

"Board what?" asked Mee. There was one lonely ship in the harbor. It was a beautiful sailing ship with a figurehead of a young woman, naked to the waist, with golden hair, blue eyes, and pink cheeks.

"That's the ship we came on," said the footmen. They got out of the coach and walked across the quay to the mooring place.

On board there was no one to be seen. They walked up the gangway and looked in the wheelhouse, the forecastle, the cabin, and the hold. Then they went to the harbor tavern to ask what had happened to the crew.

"They were recruited," said the landlord of the tavern. "They had never been anywhere on the mainland but the harbor towns, and adventure was calling to them. The men wanted to see the world, win riches, fall in love. An army captain offered them good pay, so they left."

Mee was trembling. His heart had been bleeding since he had breathed in the scent of dune roses and sea wind, heard the sound of the surf and the swirling sand, and seen the mussel beds and the white-crested waves. He kept seeing the sorrowful face of his mother before him, which he had been unable to brighten even with his most beautiful song.

"We'll eat, we'll sleep, and then we'll go back," he said. "We can't get to the island without a ship, and I'm not staying here for a day longer than necessary."

"There's a skipper who lives in the town," said the landlord. "A master seaman. His name is Gawein. Maybe he will take you over to the island."

He directed them to Gawein's house, and after dinner they headed there. It was a very small house, with a shed alongside where wooden figureheads and other ship carvings could be seen through the large windows: mermaids, savage crocodiles, and a whole series of statues of the same tall and wiry sailor.

From the house came a plaintive song. They stopped for a moment to listen. ·

When the horse sees the stable
He'll gallop and snort

But the sailor's heart races
In sight of the port . . .

Mee knocked at the door.

"Come in!" called a deep voice.

The sailor Gawein was sitting beside a bed upon which a fragile blond woman was lying, with her eyes closed. "She has just passed away," he said, his voice catching in his throat. "Please sit down." He did not stand, but remained sitting beside the bed, his large hand upon the small hand of his departed wife.

"She has been very ill," he said. "Now she is better."

"We need a skipper," said Mee, his voice full of compassion, "but we won't disturb you any further."

"The sea is calling," said Gawein. "She has been calling me for a long time now. I have a figurehead to deliver for the ship belonging to the king of the island across the water. With that money and what's here, I can buy a ship and pay a crew and take you where you want to go."

"We need to go to the island across the water, and we have a ship," said Mee.

"Give me three days," said Gawein.

"If you're seeking a singer of sorrows," said Mee, "now that we're here anyway . . ." He looked at the pale face on the pillow, and tears began to roll from his eyes.

"You are Mee, the singer of sorrows," said Gawein. "Your name and fame resound over land and sea, from Trondheim to Lisbon and from Riga to Smyrna. Many a crew that has lost a shipmate and surrendered the body to the waves has longed for your consolation."

Already, Mee could no longer hear his words. He was singing a strange and semi-comprehensible song in a tune that lay betwixt, beside, and beneath the usual melodies, a tune that nobody would have been able to sing after him.

"Sailor's sweetheart, sailor's sweetheart," came his plaintive voice.

Gawein shivered.

The Sailor's Sweetheart

She was a carpenter's daughter. She had blond hair and blue eyes, and she was small and dainty. Her name was Brettele. Her sister Antinua had brown eyes and black hair, and she was short and sturdy.

Brettele worked in her father's furniture workshop. She carved the lions' heads to decorate the arms of the chairs, and the garlands of roses for the lids of the Langstrand bridal chests. Antinua helped her mother in the garden and in the yard, churning the milk, taking the honey from the comb, and weeding the vegetable garden.

Every Saturday evening, the sisters would go dancing at the sailors' inn in Langstrand. Antinua would dance with her intended, a farmer's son. Brettele would dance with anyone who wanted to dance. She loved music and her nimble feet could follow any rhythm, but she didn't feel the arms that the sailors and the farmers' sons would put around her waist, and she didn't hear the sweet words that they would whisper in her ear.

One evening, when Antinua was whirling around with her farmer's son, a sailor asked Brettele to dance. He was tall and wiry, just as a sailor should be, and when he took her in his arms and swung her around, Brettele felt as though she were in a huge ship surging through the towering waves of the ocean.

"Never marry a sailor," said Antinua as they were walking home that night. "A sailor loves only the sea."

"And your farmer's son loves only his land," teased Brettele.

"At least he's always nearby," said Antinua. "In the morning you milk the cows together, in the afternoon you both till the land, and in the evening the two of you take care of the animals and the poultry, and you clean the yard together. When you marry a farmer, you're never alone again."

Brettele said nothing. She was thinking about the strong arms of the sailor, which had picked her up and whirled her around as though she were a feather, and about his muscular thighs and his large hands. His skin was brown and weather-beaten and his eyes were deep and dark, and when he looked at her they glowed. He had black curls that were all of a tangle, as though there were no comb capable of undoing the work of the sea wind that blew through them every day. He smelled of salt and tar and, although she wasn't sure why, of horses' bodies steaming in the winter.

The next evening Brettele returned to the sailors' inn.

"What are you thinking of?" asked Antinua. "It's Sunday evening. The farmers have to get up early again tomorrow and the fishermen are putting out to sea. This is no evening for dancing."

But Brettele's sailor was there, and they danced the whole evening without saying a word. When he held her in his strong arms, it seemed as though she were floating through the skies on a cloud. The gentle breath from his nostrils made the blond hairs on her neck stand shivering on end.

When they were outside, taking their leave by the light of the moon, Brettele heard his voice for the first time.

"What is your name?" he asked, taking hold of her hands.

Brettele felt as though she suddenly had twenty fingers instead of ten, and she swayed a little.

"Brettele," she said in a quavering voice.

"My name is Gawein. I'm sailing to Riga tomorrow for wood, grain, hemp, and tar. What shall I bring back for you?"

"A block of wood," said Brettele.

"I'll bring you back a block of wood from Riga," said Gawein, "and then we'll get married."

"All right," said Brettele.

Gawein took out a handful of gold pieces. "Rent a little house and furnish it," he said.

"All right," said Brettele. She stowed the money away.

Gawein took hold of her hands once again. His fingers on hers were scorching hot. "I have to go on board," he said. He let go of Brettele and turned around.

For a moment she felt as though, instead of twenty fingers, she had none at all. The gentle night air had suddenly become chilly around her shoulders. She shivered and ran back home.

A few months later, they celebrated a double wedding. Brettele and Antinua were married on the same day to keep the costs down. They danced the whole evening, and it was not only Brettele's feet that stamped in time with the music, her heart beat along with it too. When she was whirling around in Gawein's arms, she thought she could feel the earth spinning. His hand on her back was so hot that it felt as though her skin were melting, and she was surprised that his fingers did not just slide straight through her.

Antinua and her bridegroom Rudroch left the party early. Rudroch had bought a farm not far from Langstrand, and his parents had given him a horse and cart.

"You're not in any hurry to leave," said Antinua to her sister.

"No," said Brettele. "I'm not in any hurry. Wherever Gawein is, I want to be there too, no matter where it might be."

Only after the last of the guests had left did Brettele and Gawein go to their house, which stood in the center of Langstrand. When Brettele had turned the key in the lock, Gawein pushed the door open with his foot and carried her over the threshold. Brettele felt as though she were sitting on a flying star that was shooting through the heavens.

Gawein had a few weeks' leave. Every evening Brettele and her bridegroom would go dancing at the sailors' inn until the last of the guests had disappeared, and every evening Gawein would carry his bride over the threshold of their house.

"I'm going to Bilbao for iron and wool," said Gawein when his leave was over. "What shall I bring back for you?"

"Wool for knitting," said Brettele, blushing.

Once Gawein had put out to sea, Brettele went to visit her sister.

"You don't look too good," said Antinua. "I warned you. Never marry a sailor."

"When he picks me up, I feel as though I'm an angel floating through the air," said Brettele. "Do you feel the same way?"

Antinua showed Brettele the clean yard and the brick-paved space in front of the farmhouse, where Rudroch had placed a beautiful white rocking chair. "When I'm tired in the evening, I sit down and rock in my chair," said Antinua. "That's all the floating I need."

Once she was back in her house, Brettele took out the chisels and gouges that she had brought from her father's workshop. She fixed the block of wood from Riga to the kitchen table with her vise and began to chop away at it.

Every day she would go to the carpenter's workshop to help her father, and every evening after dinner she would take the chisel to the block of wood and work on the statue of her sailor. When she missed Gawein's arms around her, she took a finely sharpened knife and cut out the muscular upper arms and shoulders. When she was sad and thought he would never return, she used the smallest gouge of all to carve his eyes and mouth. When she was angry at the sea for taking her husband away, she used the big chisel to hack the folds into his sailing trousers.

One day flowed into the next like waves upon the shore, until finally the day came when Gawein's ship sailed into the harbor. Brettele had been on the lookout all day. As he walked down the gangplank, she waved to him with both arms and called his name. Gawein put down his bags and bundles and waved back.

When he reached her and put down his bags and bundles once again so that he could swing her around in his strong arms, Brettele thought she was floating into heaven on a cloud and that the angels were singing for her. But it was Gawein's song.

> *When the horse sees the stable*
> *He'll gallop and snort*
> *But the sailor's heart races*
> *In sight of the port . . .*

And she felt his heart thumping in his chest, more slowly and heavily than her own.

For the third time Gawein put down his bags and bundles so that he could carry Brettele over the threshold of the house. But this time, when he held her in his arms, she didn't think that she was in a ship that was surging through the towering waves of the ocean. She laid her face against his shoulder and no longer imagined that she was floating through the skies on a cloud. She closed her eyes. She didn't think of a flying star that was shooting through the heavens. When he put her down and she swayed as she held on to him, she understood. There was no ship, no cloud, and no star. It was only the arms of her husband Gawein that had carried her over the threshold of their house. That was all. And it made her feel giddy.

"I'm going to London for coal and lead," said Gawein when it was time. "But I'll bring back a block of wood for you so that you can make a figurehead for my ship, because you're the best wood-carver any sailor's ever seen."

Brettele blushed. "I'll knit until you get back," she said.

In the daytime Brettele helped out in her father's workshop, and in the evening she knitted baby clothes: little pullovers, cardigans, trousers, and jackets. Sometimes she would visit her sister, who would be sitting with her round belly in the rocking chair in front of the house.

"You look cold and lonely," Antinua would say. "I told you not to marry a sailor. A sailor loves only the sea."

"When I think of him, I'm not cold," said Brettele. "I only have to see his face before me or look at my wooden sailor statue and I start to glow. Do you glow when you think about your husband?"

"We've had the very best and most expensive wood-burner installed in the kitchen," said Antinua proudly. "We don't have to be cold ever again."

Brettele gave her all the clothes she'd knitted. "I don't need them for the time being," she said.

"A sailor's never there when you need him," said Antinua. "I'm going for a nap now, because it's hard work carrying a baby inside you."

The days and nights without Gawein were endlessly long for Brettele, but when the ship finally sailed into harbor and she heard his voice singing the same song as before, she forgot her sadness and loneliness.

Gawein put down his bags and bundles to wave to her. Then he put them down again to take her in his arms, and he put them down for a third time to carry her over the threshold of their house. When he held Brettele in his arms and pressed her face into his sweater, she knew that this was the moment she'd been waiting for all those weeks. It was worth all of those lonely nights and days to lie in Gawein's arms like this and to float over the threshold of their house. And when he put her down, she felt giddy.

"Let me see what you've knitted," said Gawein when they'd finished eating and he'd given her the block of wood to make a figurehead for his ship.

"I gave it all to Antinua," blushed Brettele. She lowered her eyes. "We don't need the clothes."

"All right," said Gawein. "You'll be able to spend all of your time on the figurehead. I want you to make a mermaid, naked to the waist, with golden hair and roses in her cheeks, but she's not to look like you. I don't want the whole crew of the ship and all of the pilots and dockers in foreign harbors to be looking at you."

"All right. I'll do it," said Brettele.

"I'm going to Smyrna for silk and carpets," said Gawein when it was time. "I shall bring back another block of wood for you so that you can make a mast board and a decorated ship's wheel, because you're the best wood-carver any sailor's ever seen."

"Bring back a carpet for me as well," said Brettele. "The house gets cold in winter."

It was the worst winter for years. During the day, Brettele helped out in her father's workshop, and in the evening she kept herself warm by working on the figurehead, which she made in her sister's likeness. Sometimes she would go to see Antinua, who had tightly bundled up her child in the clothes that Brettele had knitted.

"I told you not to marry a sailor," said Antinua. "Just take a good look at yourself. You're always alone. I can talk with my husband and my child all day. Who listens to you?"

"When I go to the sea," said Brettele, "the waves tell me how Gawein is and they carry my greetings to him."

"Then the waves will have told you that his ship is stuck in the ice at Witstrand, won't they?" said Antinua.

Brettele blushed and went to her father's workshop.

"Father, lend me your horse and cart," she said. "I'm going to call on my husband."

Her father loaded up the cart with boxes and chests to be delivered along the way. Brettele carefully packed her figurehead in a Langstrand bridal chest, which she filled with wood shavings. The figurehead was just finished, and she wanted to surprise Gawein with it.

The journey took two days. It was cold sitting up front; snow and ice blew into Brettele's face, but she thought about Gawein's warm hands and didn't notice the cold at all. She spent the first night at an inn, but on the second day she carried on traveling until, in the evening, the smell of tar from the shipyard in Witstrand, mingled with the smell of burning from the smokehouses, entered her nostrils.

Her horse started trotting faster, as though it fancied a bit of smoked eel for dinner.

Full of anticipation, Brettele drove into Witstrand. She left the cart outside the harbor inn and stepped over the threshold.

In the inn there was a thick fug of soot, smoke, and steaming bodies. It muffled the shouts of the sailors and the accordion music. Brettele waited until she became accustomed to the haze and looked around to see if she could spot Gawein.

Beyond the bar was a raised platform where cabin boys and harbor girls were dancing. Gawein was not among them.

Around the large fire in the center of the room were wooden benches where sailors were sitting with ladies of pleasure in their arms. Gawein was not among them.

Brettele was afraid that he'd stayed behind on his boat and that she wouldn't be able to see him that evening. Her heart thudded with disappointment, and she began to feel cold, in spite of the stuffy heat that was filling the room.

Around the walls were large corduroy smoking chairs with little tables in front of them. The helmsmen, the skippers, and the bosuns sat there, with scantily dressed ladies on their laps. Gawein was not among them.

Brettele turned around with tears in her eyes. She would have to ask the innkeeper for a place to sleep and go in search of Gawein tomorrow.

Then she saw him. He came reeling in through a side door, followed by a large, ruddy woman who looked as though she hadn't had time to dress herself properly. Her hair was hanging around her face, loose and slovenly; the top of her dress was half undone, and her feet were bare. Gawein's hair was all of a tangle as well, as though no comb could compete with the sea wind that blew through his curls every day. His sweater was on back to front and his bootlaces were undone. His cheeks were flushed in the way that Brettele knew so well, and as soon as the two of them were through the door, he put his arm around the woman and kissed her on the lips. Then he looked around.

At that moment Gawein saw Brettele. He let go of the woman and opened his mouth. Brettele dashed to the door and ran away, into the narrow lanes of Witstrand. She heard Gawein calling her name.

Brettele ran past the eel smokehouse and the shipyard, Gawein's footsteps thudding behind her. Then she heard a thump and a curse. In her mind's eye, she saw the loose laces of Gawein's boots, and she slowed her pace. She hid in a shed where fishing nets were stored for the winter and watched as he ran past. Much later she crept back to the harbor inn, untied her horse, and drove the cart away.

The inn where she'd spent the night on the way to Witstrand was too far. When she became too tired to carry on, she stopped. She covered the horse with two blankets. She took the figurehead out of the bridal chest where she'd stored it for transport, and she lay down in the chest herself, with her knees drawn up, and covered herself with wood shavings. Shivering, she tried to get to sleep.

Early in the morning she drove on without eating or drinking and delivered the packages and chests for her father as she went, because she'd been too impatient to do it on the way there. She also delivered the Langstrand bridal chest. She left her figurehead lying loose in the cart, where it rolled to and fro on every sharp bend.

When she arrived at her father's workshop, she stabled the horse and put away the cart in silence. That night, in her cold house, she couldn't warm herself up again. She spent the following days ill in bed.

When she had recovered from her illness, she fastened the figurehead to the table and carved away at the wood until Antinua's face had become hers and her sister's upper body had changed into her own. Then she touched up the paintwork and left the figurehead to dry.

The thaw set in, spring arrived, and Gawein came home. Brettele was too weak to go to the harbor. She waited for him in front of the house. Gawein put down his bags and bundles and picked her up. Brettele laid her face against his sweater and closed her eyes. And she floated over the threshold like that. It was not a happy kind of floating, like at the fair, but a slow and mournful floating, like that of a sick woman on a litter.

"That's a beautiful figurehead," said Gawein after dinner. "You've made it look like you and now the whole crew of the ship will look at you. Pilots and dockers in foreign harbors will admire you when they see my ship come in. But I asked you not to carve it in your own likeness, didn't I?"

"Indeed you did," said Brettele.

Gawein sighed. "You knew that you were marrying a sailor," he said. "A sailor belongs to the sea." He looked at Brettele.

Brettele went weak at the knees when he looked her right in the eyes, and she nodded.

"When a sailor's been sailing on the ocean for weeks and land comes into view, then all he wants to do is stretch his legs and walk on dry land. And then he has to go out drinking, because the order and discipline on a ship are so stifling, and every once in a while a sailor has to cast off his anchor." Gawein looked at Brettele, willing her to understand him.

Brettele felt her heart melting and she nodded.

Gawein put his arm around her and she felt giddy. She wanted to cling on to him and keep him with her forever.

"When a sailor's been out drinking with his shipmates, then his legs want to dance, and he wants to hold the harbor girls in his arms and swing them around." Gawein had tears in his eyes.

Brettele brushed his tears dry with her hand and nodded.

"And then he remembers how long he's been lying alone in his cage of planks without anyone to hold or to kiss, while his wife is at home cuddling and caressing her children."

Brettele remained silent.

"If a sailor can't kiss and cuddle a harbor girl when he's on shore," said Gawein, "then he shouldn't go out dancing with his shipmates. And if he can't dance with his shipmates, he shouldn't go to the harbor inn to drink and cast off his anchor. If a sailor can't cast off his anchor, then he shouldn't go on shore to stretch his legs. And a sailor who doesn't go on shore from time to time to stretch his legs can't manage life on board. A sailor who can't manage life on board has to return to dry land and set up shop as a ship chandler."

Gawein fixed his gaze on Brettele. "If you want me to return to dry land and work as a ship chandler, I'll do it. I'll be able to carry you over the threshold every day, and we can be together day and night. I'll forget about the sea."

"It's time for bed," said Brettele. She put the carpet that Gawein had brought from Smyrna on the floor beside the bed, then wrapped herself up in a blanket and lay down on it.

"Come to bed," said Gawein.

"Husband and wife sleep in a bed," said Brettele, "but a sailor is married to the sea and the seafaring life. I can't be your wife — I'm your sailor's sweetheart. Come here."

From then on, Gawein and Brettele slept on the carpet from Smyrna.

"I'm going to Naples for wine and marble and oil," said Gawein when it was time. "What shall I bring back for you?"

"Bring back a block of wood for me," said Brettele. "I'm going to open up a shop selling carvings for ships. There's a lot of demand for mast boards and decorated ship's wheels, for figureheads and leeboards with carved decorations. You need money so that you can go on shore and drink and dance and kiss the harbor girls, because you can't get all of those things for free. I need money for the rent and my paint and tools."

"All right," said Gawein. "When I come back I'll bring wood for you, and I'll put down all my bags and bundles to carry you over the threshold. I'm married to the sea, but you're number two, and I won't carry anyone other than you over the threshold."

"All right," said Brettele.

When Gawein was away, Brettele didn't help in her father's workshop anymore, but she carved and hacked away all day to stock up on carvings for her shop. She carved crocodiles with snapping teeth, dragons with flashing fangs, and evil women with snakes in their hair, and even the flowers in the borders had long tongues for catching insects. She sold everything that she made, because sailors are superstitious, and they think that having terrifying animals, evil women, and carnivorous flowers on their ship will scare away disaster.

Sometimes Brettele would go to visit Antinua, who was usually sitting in the rocking chair with her child on her lap. Chickens and rabbits and piglets would be scratching about in the yard and Rudroch, her husband, was always nearby.

"I told you not to marry a sailor," said Antinua. "A sailor loves the sea above all else."

"You're right," said Brettele, and she took her nephew from Antinua. "But I'm number two, and that's worth something. And when he comes on shore and takes me in his arms, I float straight to heaven."

"I'd rather not think about Rudroch taking me in his arms," said Antinua, rubbing her hand over her round belly. "There'll soon be more than enough mouths to feed on the farm, and I don't have time for floating anyway."

On Saturday Brettele went to the harbor inn just as she had done before she met Gawein. *I'm not a married woman,* she said to herself, *and on Saturday evening single girls go out dancing.*

She closed her eyes as she whirled around and imagined that it was Gawein holding her in his arms, because the hands of the sailors and the cabin boys had no weight and she didn't feel their touch. And she always went over the threshold of the harbor inn on her own.

And so the years passed, until Gawein went to Trondheim for stockfish, cod-liver oil, and copper, and didn't return. Brettele had used up all of the wood that he'd brought and still his ship hadn't returned to the harbor.

"He's married his sea once and for all," said Antinua. "I told you not to marry a sailor, didn't I? He's got another sweetheart in another town and a bunch of poor little mites and he's never going to come back to you."

"But I have a lifetime's worth of memories of him," said Brettele, "and when I think of him my head fills with music."

"We're going to a wedding for farming folk on Saturday, with bagpipes and hurdy-gurdies," said Antinua. "That's all the music I need."

Brettele ordered wood from the city and carried on working. Her ship carvings became well-known even in distant lands, and orders came in from far and wide. Her arms grew muscular from all of the hacking and carving. She had enough money for a bigger and better home, but she didn't want to leave Gawein's house, and any money she had over she gave to Antinua, who now had five little mouths to feed.

One day, when Brettele had sat down for a short rest, she heard a strange thumping sound in the lane where her house stood. She went to the doorway and saw a man approaching in the distance.

At first she thought it was Gawein and her heart raced with joy, but then she remembered that there was no news of a ship coming in. She took another good look. The man had a wooden leg that tapped on the cobbles with every step he took. He had a scruffy, grizzled beard and curls that the constant sea wind had blown into a permanent tangle that no comb or brush could ever tame.

It was Gawein.

"You've been away for a long time," said Brettele when he was standing before her. She looked down at his wooden leg. "Is that the piece of wood you've brought me from Trondheim?"

Gawein looked at the ground. "An anchor fell on my leg," he said. "I got gangrene in it. I didn't dare come back to you."

"I've never been scared of a piece of wood," said Brettele.

"I've lost my ship," said Gawein. "I've come to you with empty hands." He turned away from her and made to leave.

"Where are you going?" asked Brettele.

"The worst thing of all," mumbled Gawein, his face turned away, "the worst thing of all is that I can't carry you over the threshold."

"You do want to carry me over the threshold then?" asked Brettele. Her heart was thumping.

"That's what I always dreamed of," said Gawein. "On the sea, on land, in storms and in heat waves, by day and at night, in the harbor and away from the shore, I always thought about how I would carry you over the threshold and how you would lie with your head on my chest and then sway just a little when I put you down."

"Then there's only one thing for it," said Brettele. She picked up Gawein in her strong arms and carried him over the threshold. She pushed the door shut with her foot. With him still in her arms, she walked through the room and up the stairs until she was standing before the bed. There she laid him down.

"Now you're divorced from the sea," she said, "even though I don't know for how long. But right now I'm your wife." She stretched out beside him. "We can sleep in the bed."

The Carpenter's Husband

By the time Mee had finished singing, it was deep into the night.

They sat together in silence for a while. Mee coughed and cleared his dry throat.

"What happened to your leg?" Mitou finally asked Gawein shyly. She was wearing a yellow skirt with blue roses on it, and she traced the petals with her finger so she wouldn't have to look at Gawein.

Gawein let go of his wife's hand and knocked on his wooden leg. "A fight," he said after a while. "That's how it happened. A drunken seamen's fight." He sighed. "About a woman."

He stood up and limped off to fetch a glass of water for Mee.

"She was the helmsman's girl," he said when he came back. "When he heard that she was carrying my child, he dropped the heavy anchor on me when I was standing on the quay. He didn't want his girl anymore; she didn't want me anymore. I got a wooden leg and I was sunk."

Gawein looked at his wife. "She always waited for me with open arms. 'You must go back to sea, on your own ship,' she said when I came back to her as a cripple. 'We can make a lot of money from my work. If you help me with the sales and delivery, you can buy a new ship in a few years and go to sea and pay for everything that life at sea entails. Because the girls in the harbor inns aren't as cheap as I am.' And then she laughed and kissed me."

Gawein looked at Brettele and a tear ran down his cheek. "She wasted away when I stayed on shore," he said, "even more than I did. One day she asked me to go dancing with her at the harbor inn. I danced as best I could. I held Brettele in my arms, and her eyes were closed. She was pale. At night we walked to the beach and sat on a dune. 'You must go to sea soon,' she said to me. 'Don't wait any longer. Look for a ship.' She cuddled up to me, but she was still trembling.

" 'I loved your breath,' she said, 'because I could hear the sound of the sea in it. I loved the tide that crashed in the thumping of your heart. I loved the waves that picked me up when you held me in your arms. Because a sailor's wife loves the sea above all else, and her husband is number two.' I laughed, but she wasn't joking. 'Since you've left the sea, the sea has left you,' she said. 'I can't love a ship chandler.' Then I knew that I would have to hurry, or I would lose both the sea and the love of my wife. But it was already too late."

They sat together in silence. "And where will you go on your first journey?" asked Mee finally.

"To take the figurehead to the king," said Gawein.

"Our ship has a figurehead like that too," said Mee. "It is a young woman, naked to the waist, with magnificent . . ." He looked at the face of Gawein's wife. "Actually . . ."

He couldn't finish his sentence. Gawein stumbled out of the house.

"Stay here," said Mee to Mitou. He ran after Gawein. It was not far to the harbor. Gawein was staring at the ship with the blond woman on the prow — his wife, his ship.

"I'll buy you back," he mumbled. "Even if it costs me everything we've got."

He turned to Mee. "After I've sailed to the island," he said, "I'll go in search of my child. I don't care about the woman, but I want to see the child." He screwed up his eyes and looked out over the sea. "Do you know why the sailor's heart races in sight of the port?" he asked.

"No," said Mee.

"His heart races because he is happy to see his woman. And his heart trembles with the fear that he will stay with her and not return to the sea as a free man. The heart of a sailor chases backwards and forwards between these two poles, constantly to and fro."

"Not anymore," said Mee gently. "Now there is only the sea." He realized that his own heart also had two poles: his fear of seeing the coast again, and his longing to return to the dunes and bring the memory of his mother back to life. In the half-light of the harbor, he saw her beloved face before him, and the smile with which she had always looked at him. It was the tender smile of a mother looking at her child. It was not the radiant smile with which she had looked at Mee's father. A thought began to buzz around in Mee's head, as insistently as a hornet.

"Come on," he said to Gawein. "There's still a lot to do."

The Princess in the Mirror

It was a beautiful funeral. Brettele's coffin came from her father's workshop and was decorated with carved flowers. Mee sang his sorrowful song, Brettele's ancient father reminisced about his favorite daughter, and her sister spoke a few words beside the grave.

"I'll keep it brief," she said. "She should never have married a sailor."

The farmers and their wives nodded stiffly, arm in arm, of one accord, just as they worked as a couple to keep the yard clean, milk the cows, and till the land. The sailors' wives whose men were out at sea stood alone, and the lucky ones whose men were on dry land stood beside their husbands, a short distance away, with the sea wind between the two of them. They gently shook their heads, but said nothing.

"Where is Mitou?" asked Gawein when all the speeches had been made. He sought her with his eyes.

Mitou was standing right at the back. She was wearing a pale blue jacket with a dark blue checked skirt, because she had no clothes that were more appropriate for a funeral ceremony.

"Play some seamen's shanties for us, Mitou," urged Gawein. "My wife, who was my sweetheart, loved dancing and cheerful music."

Mitou stepped forward hesitantly and played "No Red Roses on a Sailor's Grave," "Would You Marry a Man Who Married the Sea?" and other shanties. To his annoyance, Mee noticed that none of those present could keep their feet still, not even Rudroch and Antinua.

Then Gawein bared his head and let the wind play through his tangled curls, which no comb had ever tamed. "I have picked you up for the last time, my sweetheart, my wife," he said. "Number one is the sea, but you are number two, and never will I carry another over the threshold."

"A likely story," muttered Antinua, but her words were drowned out by the women sobbing and the men clearing their throats.

The crewmen of the ship had also come to the funeral, and when everything had been taken care of, the figurehead packed for the king, the furniture covered to await Gawein's return, and the house locked up, they fetched the three footmen and their carriage from the inn and boarded the ship.

Once they were out on the open sea, the eldest footman spoke.

"We have come up with all manner of plans and schemes to cure our king's daughter," he said sadly. "Court jesters and clowns have visited to put a smile on her face, and she did smile a little, but she still remained sitting in front of the mirror, just looking at herself."

"A storyteller came from a hot and distant land," said the second footman. "He drummed upon a large wine cask and translated what the cask had to say. The king's daughter listened most attentively, and when the storyteller left she shook his hand, but she still remained sitting in front of the mirror, just looking at herself."

"There was no remedy for her suffering," said the third footman.

Mitou was shivering. She pulled her orange-and-purple-striped shawl a little more tightly around her shoulders, to keep out the strong gusts of sea wind. No one said another word.

"Land ahoy!" cried Gawein after some hours' sailing. He handed the helm to one of his shipmates and joined the others. His cheeks had a fresh glow, and he was rubbing his hands in satisfaction. "Ah, nothing tops the sea," he said. Then his gaze fell upon the figurehead of his dead wife and his face grew somber. He looked up at the albatross that was flying along with the ship. "Well, except for the occasional albatross flying above it, of course," he said and smiled.

When they had moored in the island's harbor, Gawein took leave of Mee and Mitou. "I'm going to see the harbormaster," he said, "to ask about the owner of the ship, so I can buy her back. Then I'll wait on board for you to return from the palace, and I'll take you back to the mainland. In the meantime, I'll give my ship a name. *Her* name. *Sailor's Sweetheart.*"

Mee and Mitou made their way to the palace with the footmen.

Prince Viereg came through the gate to meet them. They bowed to him and the prince bowed back. In silence, he led them through the palace gardens and up the marble steps.

The king's daughter was still sitting in front of her mirror, just as she had done for all those years. When Mee and Mitou entered with Prince Viereg she looked at them in the mirror, and they looked back at her. Then they looked around the royal bedroom for somewhere to sit. There was a four-poster bed in the room, with golden posts and a large mirror on the ceiling above, so that the king's daughter could see herself as she went to bed at night and as soon as she woke up.

Prince Viereg sat down beside Princess Esperanza and held her hand. The king's daughter blushed, but did not withdraw her hand.

Mitou sat down on the edge of the bed.

Mee pulled up an elegant little chair with pink and blue velvet stripes and sat down beside the king's daughter, but a short distance away, so that he would be able to look at her real face, and not the reflection. He saw her from the side, just as he had seen his mother when his father was still alive and the place opposite her at the table did not belong to Mee.

He looked and he looked and he looked. The king's daughter had dark eyes, the shape of almonds, as though she were an Eastern princess. Her hair was long, black, and straight. Every now and then, she would gracefully move her small hands to push aside a lock of her hair or to push up her sleeve, and then Mee's breath would catch in his throat. Sometimes she would peep out of the corner of her eye at Mee, who kept his eyes constantly focused on the side of her face.

Mee felt no song welling up within that might provide an explanation for the strange behavior of the king's daughter. His thoughts went no further than the almost invisible golden down on her cheeks, the shape of her ears and her neck, the soft curve of her shoulders. His gaze glanced off her skin and her clothes, and he could not get through to her heart.

And yet he could not keep his eyes off her. He thought of nothing but her beauty, and he could not take possession of her soul, her story, her sorrow, and her pain. He did not see Prince Viereg, who was lavishing loving attention upon her. He paid no attention to Mitou, who was looking out of the window, her eyes following the butterflies that darted above the palace gardens. All he wanted to do was look at the princess.

They sat like that for two long days. They ate their meals in the princess's room, and in the evening they were taken to their chambers in the guest wing. All that time, the king's daughter sat perfectly still. She had difficulty even drawing breath. Now and then a single tear would roll down her cheek, and Prince Viereg would gently wipe it away. Silver beads of perspiration glistened on her brow.

On the morning of the third day she very briefly turned to Mee. "So, are you planning to do anything then?" she asked.

Mee did not answer. Her direct look, straight on, almost overwhelmed him. He lowered his eyes.

"*One, two, three, four, what are we all waiting for?*" sang Esperanza. "You might as well get on with it."

"With what?" mumbled Mee.

"Singing and dancing, telling jokes, entertaining me."

Mee pointed at Mitou. "She's the one you want for that. All I'm doing is looking at you."

The king's daughter held her breath. She closed her eyes. She saw a lawn in front of her with a little girl spinning around on it. "Look at me! Look at me!" cried the girl.

"Play, Mitou!" cried Esperanza.

Mitou stood up and played some of her very best and merriest songs: "A King Came Riding Through the Gate," "The Princess and the Pea," and "Mirror, Mirror, on the Wall." The king's daughter stood up and danced without taking her eyes from the mirror. And when Mitou had finished playing, she sat down and sighed.

"What did you say?" she asked Mee in a trembling voice.

"I didn't say anything," answered Mee. "All I'm doing is looking at you."

Then the princess leapt to her feet, knocked over the mirror, which shattered into a thousand pieces, grabbed Mee by the shoulders, and danced around with him.

"Where do you come from, boy?" asked the king's daughter when they sat down again, looking him straight in the face.

"From the land over the sea," said Mee. "I grew up by the coast, with the sound of the surf and the swirling sand, with the scent of dune roses and the sea wind, among white-crested waves and mussel beds."

"I would like to go there one day," said the princess. "I have spent so much time looking in the mirror. What I have seen does not amount to much."

"You think so little of what you have seen?" said Mee. "I have traveled far and wide. I have been to the mountains, where snow-covered peaks glisten in the sun and the laughter of brown-tanned shepherd boys echoes through the ravines. But that is nothing beside the sheen of your hair and the melody of your voice."

"Oh," said the princess, lowering her eyes.

Mitou stood up. She looked at Mee and Esperanza, who were happily talking and looking at each other, and she ran out of the royal bedchamber.

Nobody noticed that Mitou had disappeared. Prince Viereg was looking in delight at the shards of broken mirror. He took a gold ring with diamonds from his finger and pressed it into Mee's hand. "Do not refuse," he whispered insistently. "You're going to need it."

Princess Esperanza had eyes and ears only for Mee.

"I have been in the forests," he said, "where soft moss covers the ground and wide-eyed deer stand still in your path. But all that pales beside the twinkle in your eyes and the tinkle of your laugh."

The face of the king's daughter shone with joy.

"I have traveled through marshlands," said Mee, "where slender boats nose their way through the reeds, where moorhens and grebes make their comical dives. But all of that beauty vanishes . . ."

But then something stopped him. Mee thought hard. He twisted the royal ring round and round and finally slid it onto his finger. He no longer knew what he wanted to say.

Prince Viereg took Princess Esperanza by both hands so that she had to look directly at him. His voice trembled with love and longing. "All of that beauty vanishes in the depths of your eyes and fades away in the scent of your skin."

"Exactly," mumbled Mee, "that's what I meant."

But nobody was listening to him.

"Will you marry me?" asked Prince Viereg. "I have waited a long time for you."

"Yes," said Esperanza.

"Yes what?" asked Prince Viereg.

"Yes, Prince Viereg," said Esperanza. "You have waited a long time for me."

"Will you marry me?" asked the prince.

"Yes," whispered the princess.

Once again, Mee was overcome by a great feeling of calm, a sense of relief, even more intensely than when the old footman had told him the princess's story and he had felt his burden start to lift.

Mee had accomplished his task on the island. He had cured the king's daughter. But he knew now that her radiant smile was not meant for him, just as his mother's radiant smile had not been meant for him. The vague thought that had been buzzing around in his head like a hornet was taking shape. He could not have made his mother happy in the way that his father had, not even if she had heard his singing. Making her happy was not his job. The sadness in her eyes was not his fault.

Mee went to the window and looked at the world outside. The grass was green, the sky was blue, the birds were singing, and the flowers were blooming. The world was as beautiful as Mitou had told him, Mitou in her colorful clothes that had so annoyed him, with her cheerful tunes and her laughing eyes. . . . He turned to look at the four-poster bed.

Mitou had disappeared.

Mee's heart began to race. He ran out of the princess's bedroom, down the stairs and along the corridors, until he was standing at the top of the steps and could see out over the palace gardens and the road to the harbor. There was no sign of Mitou in the fields or on the roads. Which way had she gone?

Mee ran down the palace's marble steps. Perhaps Mitou had gone for a walk in the palace gardens to look at the deer and listen to the birds. Perhaps she might appear at any moment, lift up her accordion, and play one of her dreadfully cheerful little tunes. Why had he detested them so much? Mee remembered the funny little songs that he used to sing himself, about the sun and the sea and the curly heads of the schoolchildren to whom he gave music lessons. When had his joy turned to misery?

Suddenly he saw his father's face in profile, as he had seen him at the table in the days of happiness and good cheer. "Father," he said, automatically talking in sign language, "how do you do this kind of thing? I mean, how do you talk to girls? What should I say? I know nothing about her. I didn't want to pay her any attention. But now I want to see her true colors, to strip away the layers, to . . ." He thought of the pink jacket with purple stripes that Mitou was wearing that day, and as he realized he might never see her and her gaudy clothes again, the color drained from his face. "What I mean, Father," he signed, "is that I want to know all there is to know about her. But I have chased her away."

He imagined his father's hands floating in the warm, shimmering air of the palace gardens. "Go swiftly, my son," the strong fingers said. "Go after her, as I did with your mother, after her, always keep going after her!"

The hands vanished into thin air. Mee took to his heels.

To the harbor, he thought. *If she's in the palace gardens I can look for her there later.* He ran the entire way. Tripping over coils of rope and anchor chains, he raced along the quay, where fishing boats and other vessels were bobbing up and down.

The mooring place where Gawein had left his ship was empty. Far in the distance he could hear a wailing sound, like the shrieking of a wounded albatross or the squealing of an out-of-tune accordion. Mee put his hand above his eyes and stared out to sea.

A ship was sailing away from the coast and turning to head southeast. The setting sun lit up the golden hair of the figurehead with fire and flame. The gilded name of the ship glittered like the light in Mitou's laughing eyes: *Sailor's Sweetheart.*

Mee shouted, "Mitou! Mitou!" But they were too distant to hear him, and she would soon be far out of reach. He could hire a fast sloop, using the prince's ring as security, and go after her as his father had urged. But if he caught up with the ship, would Mitou speak to him?

A sudden movement on the deck caught his attention — a piece of cloth whipping in the wind like a flag, flaming red, with yellow stripes and purple dots. It was a scarf of the kind only Mitou would wear. She was waving it above her head, beckoning him.

Mee waved back with both arms, and then he turned and ran. On the way to the harbor, he sang his heart out.

This book was edited by Cheryl Klein
and designed by Elizabeth B. Parisi.
The text was set in Adobe Garamond Pro,
a typeface originally designed by Claude
Garamond in the sixteenth century, and
adapted by Adobe Systems Inc.
The display type was set in Bickley Script,
designed by Alan Meeks in 1986.
The book was printed and bound
at R. R. Donnelly in Crawfordsville, Indiana.
The production was supervised
by Susan Jeffers Casel.
The manufacturing was supervised
by Jess White.